【學科能力測驗、指定科目考試、統一入學測驗、全民英檢中級適用】

英語 Make Me High 系列

Intermediate

Reading
Comprehension

英閱任我行
Global Village English
中級篇

Matthew McGinniss 著　何信彰 譯

三民書局

Ⓒ　Reading Comprehension (Intermediate)

——英閱任我行Global Village English

著 作 人	Matthew McGinniss
譯　　者	何信彰
發 行 人	劉振強
著作財產權人	三民書局股份有限公司
發 行 所	三民書局股份有限公司
	地址　臺北市復興北路386號
	電話　(02)25006600
	郵撥帳號　0009998-5
門 市 部	(復北店)臺北市復興北路386號
	(重南店)臺北市重慶南路一段61號
出版日期	初版一刷　2002年2月
	初版十一刷　2019年8月
編　　號	S 804140

行政院新聞局登記證局版臺業字第○二○○號

ISBN　978-957-14-3552-7　（平裝）

http://www.sanmin.com.tw　三民網路書店

序

英語 Make Me High 系列的理想在於超越，在於創新。

這是時代的精神，也是我們出版的動力；

這是教育的目的，也是我們進步的執著。

針對英語的全球化與未來的升學趨勢，

我們設計了一系列適合中學以上程度的英語學習書籍。

面對英語，不會徬徨不再迷惘，學習的心徹底沸騰，

心情好 High！

實戰模擬，掌握先機知己知彼，百戰不殆決勝未來，

分數更 High！

選擇優質的英語學習書籍，才能激發學習的強烈動機；

興趣盎然便不會畏懼艱難，自信心要自己大聲說出來。

本書如良師指引循循善誘，如益友相互鼓勵攜手成長。

展書輕閱，你將發現…

學習英語原來也可以這麼 High！

給讀者的話

　　恭喜您找到一項有助於提昇英文閱讀能力的最佳利器！本書由外國作家編寫，正確的英文、完整的文章結構、多樣豐富的內容和生動有趣的練習，皆能使你在無形中學會如何抓住文章重點，增進閱讀的技巧與能力，還可熟悉英文文章的寫作形式。

　　《英閱任我行》一書規劃為 Basic（基礎篇）300 字、Intermediate（中級篇）500 字、Advanced（進階篇）700 字三冊，文章的句法和用字難度逐級加深，讀者可選擇合適自己的級數加以自修學習。當您開始閱讀一個 Unit 時，請先將文章看過一次，遇到生字或不懂處可做記號標示，接著做練習題測驗自己瞭解多少。若在第一次閱讀後仍不甚瞭解文章內容，可再閱讀第二次，之後再做練習，但建議別急著翻閱 Key Words 和中譯，因為很多生字是可以根據前後文就猜出意思的，這是種很有用的英文閱讀技巧，也能更加深對生字的印象。做完練習題後別馬上參考答案，試著從文章內容中求證，證明自己可不是隨意瞎猜的唷！在此也提醒各位讀者，文章的重點多半在首段及其他段落的第一句，即主題句，這也是英文作文最常見的寫作格式。

　　《英閱任我行》提供多樣化的文章，內容涵蓋各種知識領域，讓您在閱讀英文之餘還能增廣見聞。《英閱任我行》不僅幫助您馳騁英文閱讀的世界，更引領您走進 Global Village，讓閱讀不只是閱讀，還是一種享受喔！

Table of Contents

Unit 1

The Internet

網路在手，四海遨遊！
Internet 讓世界無遠弗屆。

The Internet

The Internet is a regular part of life. Almost everyone has access to the Internet through their school, their work or at home. And even if people don't have access to the Internet at one of these places, they can always go to an Internet café. So why has the Internet become such a regular part of our lives? The reason is because the Internet is the greatest source of information ever   5
assembled.

One of the most basic parts of the Internet is electronic mail, also known as email. When you have your own email account, you can write messages to your friends, no matter where they are in the world. Email can also be sent as voice mail, meaning all you have to do is click a window on your computer to   10
hear your friend talking. With small cameras attached to your computer, you can send live images of yourself and receive images of other people. This is great fun to use among friends, but it's also valuable for businesses to use for international meetings.

Major newspapers have Internet websites updated daily. This means a   15
student in Denmark who wants to study in France can read a French newspaper and find out the news in the place where he will study. And once the student is in France, he can just as easily use the Internet to read his favorite Danish newspaper to keep up to date with the news from home. Magazines, radio stations and television stations also have Internet websites.   20
You can email a song request to the disc jockey at a radio station in another country and listen to it via speakers attached to the computer. If you log on to a television station in another country, you can watch programs that have been downloaded onto the Internet.

People who stay at home can get the feeling of travel while using the   25
Internet. By meeting foreigners in Internet rooms and visiting international websites, they can have direct contact with the whole world. For the elderly and disabled in our community, the Internet can transform a frustrating life

into an exciting life. And the Internet is the new way of doing business. For a company, a website is a cheap and interactive form of advertising. It allows customers to look over the latest information about a company, browse their entire range of product and most importantly place orders. This type of shopping is called e-commerce, and it will come to dominate our lives. $_{30}$

The number of Internet users is growing at an awesome speed and the technological breakthroughs are happening just as quickly to keep up with this demand. As the Internet grows, it is turning from a print based medium to an audio and visual based medium. This means televisions and telephones are joining computers on the Internet. With so much information available from around the world, people from everywhere are becoming very closely linked. All of these facts mean that the Internet is without doubt the number one technological breakthrough of our time. $_{40}$

Note

Multiple Choice

—— 1. Not many people can say they don't have access to the Internet ——————.

    (A) but they refuse to use it because it's inconvenient

    (B) but many people can say they have never heard of the Internet

    (C) because the Internet is a difficult concept to understand

    (D) because these days computers with Internet can be found in various places

—— 2. People who travel ——————.

    (A) get little benefit out of email

    (B) can benefit from an email account they can check from different computers

    (C) will never have any trouble meeting their friends at Internet cafés

    (D) must buy notebooks to get to the Internet

—— 3. Images and sounds can be transferred ——————.

    (A) by email

    (B) only when the receiver communicates with a disc jockey

    (C) only when the sender has access to a website and speakers

    (D) through digital camera

—— 4. For the elderly and disabled in our community, ——————.

    (A) the Internet can transform a frustrating life into an exciting one

    (B) the Internet can help them get free pizza and any other kinds of food

    (C) it is difficult to use the Internet properly

    (D) the Internet is useless because it is designed for young and able-bodied people

—— 5. The Internet is a new way of doing business because ——————.

    (A) a company can blackmail its opponent through email

    (B) customers have to pay an amount of money for browsing websites

    (C) a website is a cheap and interactive form of advertising

    (D) bargains can be made through net meeting

—— 6. The Internet is used by people —————.

    (A) to send and receive information

    (B) who are familiar with a large audience

    (C) who feel they have a disability

    (D) only for entertainment and illegal business

—— 7. E-commerce is common because it —————.

    (A) doesn't allow people to shop from home

    (B) offers people a large range of products

    (C) means people never have to do regular shopping ever again

    (D) suits people's lazy nature

—— 8. Newspapers, magazines, radio stations and television stations —————.

    (A) can use the Internet to attract an international audience

    (B) prefer not to use the Internet

    (C) update their e-commerce websites every day

    (D) love to buy special equipment through the Internet

—— 9. The Internet has grown quickly but it will probably grow even larger as more people —————.

    (A) become disabled

    (B) get frustrated with the benefits it offers

    (C) doubt that it is the number one breakthrough of our age

    (D) have access to audio and visual downloads

—— 10. People are benefiting from the Internet —————.

    (A) because they can now get any information about any person in the world

    (B) instead of the telephone and other mediums of communication

    (C) because it allows the transfer of incredible amounts of information

    (D) because they can order every meal without going out

Try This!

Jessica is interested in "Personal Email."
The I-Space Company wants to know about "Business Email."
YourNet Inc. is researching "Personal Website" use.
EveCommerce wants to learn more about "Business Website."

According to the above information, which group would be interested in the following situations?

1) Two friends using the Internet arrange a time and a place to meet.
   _____

2) A company that sends people information about a product they think will sell well. _____

3) Location on the Internet where people can find out more information about a company. _____

4) Information about a traveler's experiences that includes a number of photographs that can be viewed. _____

5) Two businessmen communicate about a deal they both want to complete.
   _____

6) An electric birthday card sent directly to your email address. _____

7) Two disabled people communicating with each other from different parts of the world. _____

8) An online newspaper that has links to sites that can sell books. _____

Key Words

account *n.* 帳號

assemble *v.* 聚集

audio *adj.* 放音的

breakthrough *n.* 突破

browse *v.* 瀏覽

click *v.* 點選

Danish *adj.* 丹麥的

demand *n.* 需求

Denmark 丹麥

disabled *adj.* 殘障的

disc jockey *n.* 電臺主持

dominate *v.* 支配

download *v.* 下載

e-commerce *n.* 電子商務

frustrating *adj.* 受挫的

interactive *adj.* 互動的

log *v.* 登入

print *n.* 印刷

speaker *n.* 揚聲器

transform *v.* 改變

update *v.* 更新

visual *adj.* 視覺的

網際網路

　　網際網路是生活中少不了的一部分，幾乎每個人從學校、上班地點或是家裡，都可以連上網際網路，而且就算在這些地方都不能使用網際網路，還是有網路咖啡店可去。那麼，網際網路為什麼會演變成日常生活中不可或缺的一部分呢？原因在於網際網路可說是有史以來資料收集最多的來源。

　　網際網路最基本的部分之一就是電子郵件，也就是email，只要有了自己的email帳號，不管你的朋友在世界的哪一個角落，你都可以寫訊息給他們。電子郵件也能以語音郵件傳送，也就是說，你只要點選一個新視窗，就可以聽到你朋友說話。電腦再加裝小型的攝影機，就可以把你自己的即時影像傳送出去，也能接收其他人的影像，不僅朋友之間使用起來格外有趣，就連做生意要開國際會議也很方便。

　　各大報也會每天更新網路上的網站，也就是說，假如丹麥有一個學生想到法國唸書，只要上網看一看法國的報紙，就可以找出他要前往就讀的地方，目前有什麼消息。而且一旦這個學生到了法國，也能利用網路，輕輕鬆鬆就可以看到他最愛看的丹麥報紙，掌握家鄉的最新脈動。雜誌、廣播電臺、電視臺也有自己的網站，你可以用電子郵件向其他國家廣播電臺的D.J.（音樂節目主持人）點歌，然後透過電腦的喇叭就可以聽到了，如果你上網連到其他國家的電視臺，還可以觀看已經放在網路上的節目。

　　一般人只要上網，就算是待在家裡也會有旅行的感覺，在網路聊天室認識外國人，或是觀看各個國家的網站，就可以和全世界直接聯繫。對社區裡的年長者以及行動不便的人來說，網路可以讓失意沮喪的生活變得多采多姿；網路也是做生意的新管道，一家公司有了網頁，就等於多了一種便宜又可以互動的廣告，讓顧客可以過目公司的最新資訊，或是瀏覽所有的產品，當然最重要的就是下單訂購了，這種類型的購物稱為電子商務，會逐漸主宰我們的生活。

上網人數的成長速度相當可觀，而科技的進步一日千里，也恰好趕得上我們的需求。經過不斷的發展，網路已經從白底黑字為基礎的媒介，演變成以影音為基礎的媒介，換句話說，電視與電話可以用網路和電腦連結起來。全世界有這麼多的資訊垂手可得，各地的人可以說是緊緊相連，這些現象意味著網際網路無疑是當代最重大的科技突破。

上網別忘記休息唷！

Unit 2

Exchange Student

當交換學生真好！
可以到國外學習，大開眼界囉！

Exchange Student

If you plan to go to university in the future, you can look forward to a great time. And if you are already a university student, you probably appreciate how much independence you have and enjoy the fact you are able to make your own choices. This freedom of choice is very rewarding, especially these days because now there is so much on offer at universities. Not only are there a wide range of courses you can study, there are also many places where you can study. If you want to take one of the greatest challenges of your life, then perhaps you should think about studying overseas as an exchange student for all or part of your course.

You should start by researching various universities. These days, it's common for exchange students to study in the United States, Canada, United Kingdom, Australia and New Zealand. If you want to study in a non-English-speaking country, you might consider France, Germany, Spain or countries in Asia such as China and Japan. When you are researching, consider the courses you can select abroad that you couldn't do at home. For example, in America you might enroll in a specialized computer or business class. In France, you might find a fashion design course and in Australia, you might find a marine biology course that is the best in the world. Undoubtedly the best place to do your research is via the Internet as most universities have their own website.

When you arrive at your new university, everything will be different from what you are used to at home. Course schedules will be strange, the living conditions will be different and the food might be disgusting. Maybe you will live in dormitories with other students. This is quite common for freshmen and sophomores in the United States and Canada. In Australia and New Zealand, it is more likely you will have your own room in an apartment. If this is not what you are used to, then perhaps you will be so shocked that you might feel like going straight back home. But be patient, after a few

5

10

15

20

25

weeks, things will begin to make sense and your initial shock will be replaced by excitement. 30

Former exchange students often said that most of their learning didn't happen in the lecture hall. That's because from the time you leave until the day you return, you will constantly be fascinated by what you see, and this is the true source of learning. Keep in mind you must be assertive. Push yourself forward instead of sitting around in your dormitory or apartment. 35 Join a club at the new university as this is one of the best ways to meet other students with similar interests. When you have a weekend free, don't just study but get out and explore your new area. Many people say that traveling and studying are the two best experiences you can have in life. When you are an exchange student, you are having both. 40

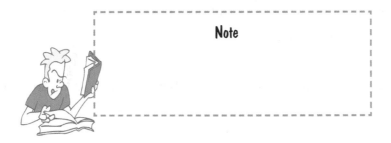

Note

True or False

———(1) University students are expected to make choices by themselves and this gives them freedom.

———(2) These days the choices for university students include what to study and where to study.

———(3) Most exchange students choose English-speaking universities because they want to do courses they can't study at home.

———(4) An exchange student may find a fashion design course in France and a marine biology course in Australia.

———(5) The Internet is a good place to research universities because it carries websites from most universities.

———(6) Often exchange students are shocked by the differences at their new university when they first arrive.

———(7) If you are not used to the new environment, you should go straight back home.

———(8) Most of the experiences and learning happen in the courses that exchange students choose to take.

———(9) Exchange students always meet people with similar interests because when they arrive, they must join clubs.

———(10) Exchange students shouldn't study because their time should be spent on traveling.

Try This!

Draw a circle around the comments you think you might hear from exchange students that have just returned home.

1) "Being an exchange student was easy because the course was taught in a different language to what I normally speak."

2) "I was able to choose the country I wanted to study in as well as the course to take."

3) "The living environment was different from what I have been used to before I left."

4) "It seems that when you meet other exchange students, they are always sophomores from America."

5) "Being assertive helped me get involved in more activities while I was an exchange student."

6) "It was disappointing being an exchange student because I never felt I learned anything."

7) "I recommend being an exchange student for a number of reasons, but I don't suggest other students should try it."

8) "The day I landed in Paris for my year as an exchange student, I began learning."

Key Words

abroad *adv.* 在國外	dormitory *n.* 宿舍	marine *adj.* 海洋的
appreciate *v.* 重視	enroll *v.* 入學	overseas *adv.* 到海外
assertive *adj.* 斷定的	exchange *v.* 交換	patient *adj.* 有耐性的
biology *n.* 生物學	fascinate *v.* 使著迷	rewarding *adj.* 有益的
club *n.* 社團	former *adj.* 之前的	schedule *n.* 時間表
constantly *adv.* 持續地	freshman *n.* 大一新生	shock *v.* 震驚
course *n.* 課程	hall *n.* 講堂	sophomore *n.* 二年級學生
disgusting *adj.* 令人厭惡的	lecture *n.* 演講	specialize *v.* 專門化

交換學生

　　假如你打算要唸大學的話，你可以期待那是一段很棒的時光；如果你已經是大學生了，你可能很珍惜現有的獨立自主，也很高興能自己做決定。可以自由選擇的確難能可貴，尤其是近年來各大學都提供許多選擇，不只選讀的課程範圍廣泛，連就讀的地方也不少。如果你想要接受生命中最重大的挑戰之一，那你或許應該考慮到國外去唸全部的課程或部分的課程，當個交換學生。

　　你應該先著手研究各個大學，近年來交換學生常到美國、加拿大、英國、澳洲、紐西蘭等國就讀，如果你想到非英語系國家唸書的話，不妨考慮法國、德國、西班牙或是亞洲國家，像是大陸和日本。在研究各大學的同時，要考慮一些你在國內修不到，但是可以到國外選讀的課程，比方說你可以到美國去上專業電腦課程或是商業課程；也可以到法國找一門時裝設計的課程；或是到澳洲去上一上世界首屈一指的海洋生物學課程。而研究的時候，透過網路無疑是最好的方法，因為大多數的大學都有自己的網站。

　　到了新學校，凡事都和你以前在國內習慣的不一樣，課表會很奇怪，生活情況也大相逕庭，食物也可能難以下嚥。也許你會和其他學生一起住宿，這對美、加兩國大一、大二的學生來說是平常事；至於在澳洲和紐西蘭，比較有可能在公寓中擁有自己的寢室。假如你不習慣這樣，那你可能會錯愕不已，很想直接飛奔回家，但是要多一點耐心，幾個禮拜過去後，一切就會步上軌道，當初的驚恐會轉由興奮取而代之。

　　以前的交換學生常說，他們大部分的知識並不是在課堂上學到的，因為從出國到回來的這段期間，你會經常對所見所聞感到著迷，這才是真正的學習方式。記住，一定要一心一意，鞭策自己向前，不要枯坐在宿舍或是公寓裡頭，要參加新大學的社團，這是很不錯的辦法，可以認識其他志同道合的學生。週末一有放假，不要只是唸書，而是要出門探索這個新天地。不少人認為行萬里路、讀萬卷書是生命中最受用的體驗，而在你做交換學生的期間，這兩者能同時享有。

交換學生的心靈點滴

　　上課剛好上到世界不同的文化，老師就出了一個題目，「你認為浪漫的夜晚可以去哪裡？做什麼？」然後把全班分成美洲學生亞洲學生歐洲學生和非洲的學生，每組派代表上台報告。亞洲的大概就是我們常聽到的那些事，像是看星星、看夜景、散步等等；美洲的說要帶瓶白酒去海邊散步；法國的學生都認為所謂的浪漫之夜一定包括高級餐廳的美食；非洲學生最勁爆了，他們根本不准有婚前約會這回事，只由雙方家長作主兩邊家庭見面就決定結婚了（見面時男女兩人還不能有eye-contact），所以不能回答老師的問題。法國和加拿大的男生都說「呵呵我們最喜歡夜晚了 (We like the dark!)」，所以後來老師問起性生活的時候，那些男生卻回答"never before marriage"，老師一臉狐疑，下面的學生也都笑成一團。

我一邊忙著適應學校的生活，一邊學著處理電話申請和銀行等從沒接觸過的事情，真正在心裡拋不開的，還是在臺灣的親友們。第一次體會什麼是思念的滋味，想念親友也想念臺灣的一切；我每天上kimo逐條閱讀臺灣新聞，連以前覺得無趣的科技財經新聞都不放過，好像硬要跟臺灣有些一絲絲的聯繫，心裡才會比較踏實。這裡雖然空氣好景色佳，連公車司機都親切熱情，但是就是少了排骨飯、少了熟悉的親人、少了臺灣又悶又黏的空氣。因為溫差過大，我連著兩三個月都在感冒，卻又隻字不敢跟媽媽提起，怕她擔心，如果咳得很嚴重，喉嚨沙啞就乾脆不打電話回家，以免拆穿。也許是我以往太不獨立了吧，其實感冒也不是什麼大病，但是我就會有那種要強逼著自己堅強的自憐，感覺以往熟悉的support group一下子完全消失，心裡空空的，連遇到有種族歧視的辦事人員也無人可陪我一起咒罵。我開始佩服那些自己在國外唸書的留學生或是獨自帶著小孩移民的媽媽，即使搬到生活品質較好的環境，身為少數族群的心理壓力和不踏實、不安全感，不是我們這種渡假性質的交換學生可以體會的。

　　上學期的我忙著適應英文環境、適應學校、適應新朋友、也適應新的自己。到了下學期，我刻意修比較輕鬆的課，讓自己更悠閒的享受美景和有趣的活動。三月維多利亞的櫻花美得像在畫裡一樣，每條街都是盛開的櫻花大道，我和幾個朋友幾乎每個週末都出去享受沙灘海邊和草原湖畔。時間一下就過去了，匆匆八個月，沮喪的時候覺得時間過得真慢，快樂的時候又希望能永遠留下來。我在心情的震盪中，學會獨立，學會不同的文化，開闊我的視野，也更深刻瞭解自己身為小島國民所養成的性格和世界觀。雖然基本的價值觀和個性沒有變，但是比較一年前的相片和現在的自己，我能夠感覺到自己已經不是原來的我了。某種程度上，我的思考模式和想法比較偏向外國人，我學會長大、學會自己獨立，我變得比較成熟也比較勇敢。我接觸到各國不同文化的學生，世界一下子變大很多，也親近很多。這也是我後來有勇氣自己跑去以色列當義工的原因，我想一年前在台灣的我，是沒有這種勇氣的。

Unit 3

Christopher Columbus

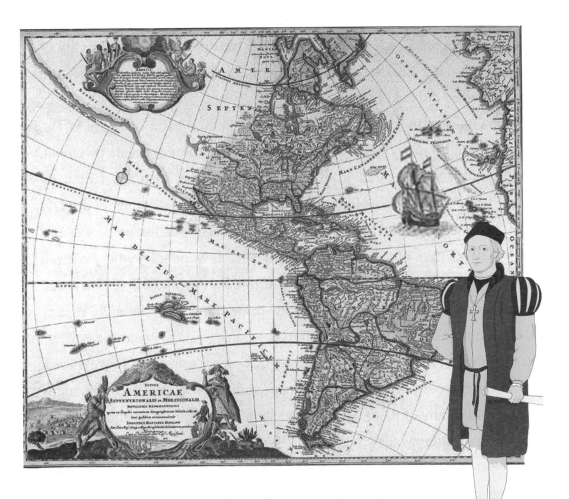

"I did not sail upon this voyage to gain honor or wealth...I came with true devotion and with ready zeal, and I do not lie."

Christopher Columbus

Christopher Columbus was the first European to discover America. In fact, before his time, Europeans didn't even know that America existed. Columbus was born in 1451 in the town of Genoa in Northern Italy. Genoa was an important port at the time and as a boy, Columbus always thought about sailing. At the age of nineteen, he got his chance and served on board 5 an Italian ship that sailed around the Mediterranean Sea. A few years later he sailed from Genoa to England on a cargo ship and later sailed from Portugal to Iceland. When he wasn't at sea, Columbus lived in the Portuguese City of Lisbon. At the time, Lisbon was the biggest port on the Atlantic Ocean and one of the busiest cities in Europe. 10

Sailors during the 1480's were exploring the West Coast of Africa, looking for gold and trying to find a way around the continent to China. Instead, Columbus suggested that it would be quicker to reach China by traveling west from Europe. He thought China was 5,600 kilometers directly west of Lisbon. But in reality, China is over 20,000 kilometers west of 15 Lisbon. The Queen of Spain was one of the few people who believed Columbus. In 1492, she provided him with three ships and all the men and supplies he needed. On August 3, 1492, the three ships, each about 25 meters long, left Spain. They first sailed south to the Canary Islands near the African coast. From there, they caught good winds that blew them quickly westward. 20 But after three weeks of sailing, the ninety sailors on board the three ships became afraid. Many of them believed the ships would never be able to return to Europe against the winds.

On October 12, land was sighted and immediately Columbus went ashore and claimed the land for Spain. The place where Columbus landed 25 was a small island called San Salvador, which today is one of the Bahamas in Central America. But at the time, Columbus believed he had discovered an island close to China. When Columbus returned to Spain, he was given a hero's welcome. The Spanish Queen was so impressed that she organized another voyage to leave as soon as possible. The second voyage left Spain in September 1493 with seventeen ships and one thousand people. The purpose was to make a Spanish settlement and find gold for Spain. But setting up the colony was difficult. Food was hard for the Europeans to produce and they had problems with the American Indians who wanted the white men to leave. 30

In 1498, Columbus made his third voyage but this time there were no volunteers to go with him and he was forced to take a crew of prisoners. In 1502, Columbus made his fourth and last voyage to America. On this last voyage, he made many important discoveries along the coast of South America. But even at this time Columbus still believed he was in Asia. In fact, it wasn't until the first voyage around the world by Magellan in 1522 that the Europeans realized the true size of the world. In 1506 Christopher Columbus died in Spain. At the time of his death, he was well known and respected as one of the greatest and bravest explorers ever to live. 35 40

Note

Multiple Choice

—— 1. Christopher Columbus was the first European —————.

    (A) to sail around the world

    (B) to discover America

    (C) who became the supporter of the Queen of Spain

    (D) whom was trusted by the Queen of Spain

—— 2. The town of Genoa influenced Columbus —————.

    (A) because it made him want to sail

    (B) because it was close to where he wanted to sail to

    (C) so much that he decided to spend many years of his life there

    (D) because it had the largest airport in Northern Italy

—— 3. After Columbus started sailing, he —————.

    (A) changed for the worse as a person

    (B) went directly to Africa

    (C) went directly to America

    (D) moved to the biggest port on the Atlantic Ocean

—— 4. Columbus thought it took too long to get to China —————.

    (A) by sailing around Africa

    (B) so he decided to search for America instead

    (C) so he decided to live in Lisbon

    (D) by ship so he decided to go by airplane

—— 5. Columbus was trusted by the Queen of Spain —————.

    (A) because he knew the exact location of China

    (B) but not by the King of Italy

    (C) because she also wanted to be a sailor

    (D) to explore the western Atlantic

——— 6. The island where Columbus first landed ——————.

    (A) is in reality close to China

    (B) does not exist anymore

    (C) is over 20,000 kilometers west of Lisbon

    (D) is very close to the American continent

——— 7. The Queen of Spain ——————.

    (A) was impressed with the gold Columbus brought back from China

    (B) helped pay for the four major voyages

    (C) went with Columbus on his last voyage

    (D) forced Columbus to take a crew of prisoners

——— 8. It was difficult to settle up the colony on the second voyage because ——————.

    (A) the wind was so strong that the crew couldn't land successfully

    (B) there wasn't enough gold to buy food

    (C) of the American Indians' defense and the shortage of food

    (D) the prisoners were rebellious

——— 9. Columbus had problems finding crew for his third voyage because ——————.

    (A) the settlement he tried to make during his second voyage was a failure

    (B) he was too friendly with the Queen of Spain

    (C) too many prisoners wanted to sail with him

    (D) he was strict and cruel to the sailors

——— 10. Columbus probably knew ——————.

    (A) exactly how big the world was at the time of his death

    (B) that Magellan would make the first voyage around the world in 1522

    (C) that he would be famous after his death

    (D) that the land he had found wasn't China

Try This!

According to the information in the article about Christopher Columbus, write down the places that match each statement.

——————— The continent that Columbus discovered by accident.

——————— The country where Columbus was born in 1451.

——————— A common destination during the 1400's for sailors wanting to find gold.

——————— The European country that believed in Columbus and provided the ships he needed to make his four major voyages.

——————— Columbus lived in this country as a young man because it featured the largest port on the Atlantic Ocean.

——————— Columbus thought he was close to discovering this country when in fact he was on an island now called San Salvador.

——————— The continent from which most voyages left to explore Africa and America.

——————— The continent where China is located.

Key Words

ashore *adv.* 到岸上
Atlantic Ocean 大西洋
Bahamas 巴哈馬群島
Canary Islands 加那利群島
cargo *n.* 貨物
claim *v.* 宣稱
continent *n.* 大陸

crew *n.* 工作人員
Genoa 熱那亞
Iceland 冰島
kilometer *n.* 公里
Lisbon 里斯本
Mediterranean Sea 地中海
Portugal 葡萄牙

prisoner *n.* 囚犯
sailor *n.* 水手
San Salvador 聖薩爾瓦多
supply *n.* 補給品
volunteer *n.* 自願者
voyage *n.* 航行
westward *adv.* 向西方

哥倫布

　　哥倫布是第一個發現美洲的歐洲人，其實在他之前，歐洲人甚至不知道有美國的存在。哥倫布於1451年出生在義大利北部的熱那亞城，熱那亞在當時是一個重要的港口，哥倫布小時候總是希望能出海航行。十九歲那年，機會來了，他在一艘義大利的船上幹活，航行於地中海各處；幾年後，他搭貨船從熱那亞航行到英格蘭；之後又從葡萄牙啟航到冰島。不出海時，哥倫布就住在葡萄牙的里斯本市，在當時，里斯本是大西洋的第一大港，也是歐洲十分繁忙的都市。

　　1480年代，大部分的水手都在非洲西岸探險，除了尋找黃金，也在找一條越過非洲大陸到達中國的水路，哥倫布反而提議，要到中國比較快的方法就是從歐洲往西行，他認為中國就在里斯本正西方五千六百公里處，可是實際上中國在里斯本西方兩萬多公里。西班牙女王是少數相信哥倫布的人，1492年，女王提供哥倫布三艘船艦，以及他所需的隨行人員與配備，1492年八月三日那天，三艘長達二十五公尺的船就這樣駛離西班牙。他們先往南航行到非洲沿岸的加那利群島，在那裡得到順風的幫助，得以快速西行；可是三週的行程過去之後，三艘船上的九十名船員開始恐慌，因為逆風，他們害怕這些船永遠回不了歐洲。

　　十月十二日，終於看到陸地了，哥倫布立刻上岸，並宣稱土地的所有權屬於西班牙，哥倫布登陸的地方其實是一個叫做聖薩爾瓦多的小島，隸屬現今中美洲的巴哈馬群島。但當時哥倫布深信他發現的是臨近中國的島嶼，回到西班牙，哥倫布受到英雄式的歡迎，西班牙女王深受感動，又儘快安排另一次航程。第二次出海是在1493年九月離開西班牙，這次一共有十七艘船隻和一千人隨行，目的是要建立西班牙的殖民地，並且替西班牙找尋黃金，可是設立殖民地困難重重，對這些歐洲人來說，食物的生產不容易，美洲的印地安人也很難應付，他們要這些白人離開。

　　1498年，哥倫布第三次出海，不過這一次沒有人自願與他同行，他只好帶領一整船的囚犯；1502年，哥倫布第四次，也是最後一次出海到美洲，最後這次的旅程中，他一路沿著南美洲航行，有許多重大的發現，不過就連這一次的航行，哥倫布依舊認為他到的是亞洲，實際上一直要到1522年麥哲倫首度繞行世界一周，歐洲人才知道世界到底有多大。1506年，哥倫布死於西班牙，過世時，他已是家喻戶曉的人物，大家對這位史上勇氣過人的偉大探險家都尊敬不已。

與眾不同的哥倫布

　　哥倫布發現新大陸之後，回到了西班牙。在一次歡迎宴會中，忽然有人高聲說道：「我看這件事不值得這樣慶祝。哥倫布不過是坐著船往西走，碰上了一塊大陸而已。任何一個人只要坐船一直向西行，都會有這個發現。」宴會席上頓時鴉雀無聲，面面相覷。哥倫布笑著站起來，順手抓起桌上的熟雞蛋說：「請各位試試看，誰能使熟雞蛋的小頭朝下，在桌上站立？」大家都拿起面前的熟雞蛋試著、滾著、笑著，但誰也沒能把它立起來。

　　哥倫布微笑著，拿起熟蛋，把尖頭往桌上輕輕一敲，蛋就穩穩地立在桌上了。那人叫道：「這不能算，他把蛋殼摔破，當然可以站立。」這時，哥倫布嚴肅說道：「對！你和我的差別就在這裡，你是不敢摔，我是敢摔。世界上的一切發現和發明，在一些人看來都是簡單不過的，然而他們總是在別人指出應該怎樣做以後才說出來。」

Unit
4 *Australia*

你知道袋鼠和無尾熊的故鄉在哪兒嗎？
我們一起一探究竟吧！

Australia

Australia is the largest island on earth. Yet for a country almost the size of the United States, Australia has a relatively small population of just nineteen million people. These days Australians come from many cultural backgrounds, and this gives Australian society a modern feel.

Most Australians live in cities. Sydney is the biggest and busiest city 5
with five million people. It features a harbor with an enormous bridge and the famous Sydney Opera House. Sydney became the center of world attention when it hosted the 2000 Olympic Games. The city is also famous for its beautiful coast of white sand beaches. Melbourne is the second largest city and is known as Australia's cultural center with its theaters, art galleries and 10
concert halls. Perth, Adelaide and Brisbane each has about one and a half million people and are clean and easy cities to live in. Darwin and Hobart are relatively small cities and so is Canberra, which is Australia's capital. Australians regard themselves as "easy-going" and are generally friendly and open-minded people. English is the major language, and over the years the 15
people have developed a distinct Australian accent.

The Aboriginal people were the first inhabitants of Australia. Recent discoveries have found parts of Aboriginal culture being one hundred thousand years old. In 1788, the British arrived and established a small colony at Sydney harbor. Life for these first white Australians was difficult, 20
and unfortunately many conflicts occurred between the old and new Australians. In 1850, gold was discovered near the southern city of Melbourne and in 1890, near the western city of Perth. This brought many new people to these areas but still life was hard on this hot and dry continent. Most of the first white Australians migrated from England, Wales, Scotland 25
and Ireland. Later, people arrived from all over Europe. In the 1950's, large numbers of people arrived from Italy, Greece and Yugoslavia. More recently, people from Asia came to live in Australia in the 1980's and 1990's.

Because it is situated in the Southern Hemisphere, Australia has summer at Christmas time and winter from June to August. For most of the year, the 30 country has warm weather and this encourages the people to spend most of their time outside. Sports such as tennis, golf, cricket, rugby and football are popular. Australians also enjoy water sports because most people live close to the ocean. Swimming, surfing, snorkeling and fishing are common, and so is going to the beach to relax and enjoy the sunshine. Most of the central, 35 western and northern parts of Australia are completely natural and great places to observe wildlife. In the spring, you can see the deserts covered with flowers, and throughout the year you can see kangaroos, koala bears, crocodiles and hundreds of varieties of colorful birds.

Australia is a great country to visit because it offers a wide range of 40 attractions. And because of its enormous size and small population, there are always places you can enjoy by yourself. Any time of the year is a good time to visit as long as you keep in mind the further north you travel, the hotter it gets.

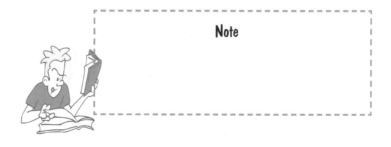

Note

True or False

——(1) Australia has a relatively small population for such a large country.

——(2) Sydney is the largest city in Australia because it is the most famous.

——(3) Perth, Adelaide and Melbourne each has a population of about one and a half million people.

——(4) Australians speak English which sounds different from the English spoken in America.

——(5) Gold was the major reason why the British set up a colony in Sydney harbor.

——(6) People from many countries have come to live in Australia and this gives Australian society a modern feel.

——(7) Most of the central, western and northern parts of Australia are completely natural and great places to observe wildlife.

——(8) In Australia, the warm weather between June and August encourages people to spend most of their time outside.

——(9) It's not difficult to be alone in Australia because of the enormous size of the country and the small population.

——(10) The further south you travel in Australia, the hotter it gets.

Try This!

Imagine you have just returned from a holiday in Australia. Answer the following questions from your friends who are planning to go there.

"If I travel to the west coast of the country which city can I visit?" _____

"Where should I go to see the site of the 2000 Olympics?" _____

"Who were the first people to live in Australia?" _____

"Can you recommend a place where I can go to galleries and the theater?" _____

"Who were the people that came to Australia in 1788?" _____

"If I visit Australia in December, which season will it be?" _____

"What do you think is the most popular activity for Australians?" _____

"If I go to Australia in July and it gets too cold, which direction should I go for hotter weather?" _____

"What do you think is the most dangerous animal in Australia?" _____

Key Words

Aboriginal *n.* 澳洲原住民

accent *n.* 口音

background *n.* 背景

colony *n.* 殖民地

conflict *n.* 衝突

cricket *n.* 板球

crocodile *n.* 鱷魚

desert *n.* 沙漠

distinct *adj.* 獨特的

easy-going *adj.* 隨和的

feature *v.* 以…為特色

harbor *n.* 港口

hemisphere *n.* 半球

host *v.* 主辦

inhabitant *n.* 居民

kangaroo *n.* 袋鼠

koala bear *n.* 無尾熊

Melbourne 墨爾本

migrate *v.* 移居

observe *v.* 觀察

occur *v.* 發生

Olympic Games *n.* 奧運會

opera *n.* 歌劇

relatively *adv.* 相對地

rugby *n.* 橄欖球

situate *v.* 坐落

snorkel *n.* 潛水

surfing *n.* 衝浪

Sydney 雪梨

variety *n.* 多樣性

Yugoslavia 南斯拉夫

澳洲

澳洲是全球第一大島，不過澳洲這麼一個幾乎和美國一樣遼闊的國家，人口卻相當稀少，只有一千九百萬人。近年來，澳洲人來自許多不同的文化背景，澳洲的社會因而充滿現代感。

大部分的澳洲人住在城市裡，雪梨是第一大城，熱鬧非凡，人口有五百萬，特色是一個海港，一座大橋，以及遠近馳名的雪梨歌劇院，雪梨主辦2000年奧運會時，成為全球關注的焦點，該市美麗的白沙海岸也相當有名。墨爾本是第二大城，劇院、美術館、音樂廳林立，是澳洲公認的文化重鎮。其他如伯斯、阿得雷德、布里斯本等地，人口在一百五十萬左右，也都是乾淨舒適、適宜人居的都市。達爾文港和荷巴特相對之下是較小的城市，澳洲首都坎培拉也是一樣。澳洲人自認他們很「隨和」，通常對人很友善、心胸也很開闊，英語是主要的語言，而且經過這麼多年，已經發展出一種特殊的澳洲口音。

原住民是最早住在澳洲的人，最近發現當地原住民的某些文化可以追溯到十萬年前。1788年，英國人來到此地，在雪梨港建立一個小型的殖民地，但早期來到澳洲的白人，日子並不好過，不幸的是，澳洲的原住民和這些新來的人發生許多衝突。1850年，南部的城市墨爾本附近發現黃金；1890年，西部的城市伯斯附近也發現黃金，吸引很多新來的人到這些地區，不過，在這麼一個又熱又乾的大陸上，日子還是不好過。早期移民到澳洲的白人，大多來自英格蘭、威爾斯、蘇格蘭、愛爾蘭等地，後來，歐洲各地的人也相繼前來，1950年代，很多人來自義大利、希臘與南斯拉夫，更晚近到了1980、1990年代，亞洲人也前來澳洲定居。

　　位在南半球的緣故，澳洲聖誕節的時候正值夏天，六月到八月反而是冬天，該國全年幾乎都是溫暖的天氣，也促使大眾多半的時間都在戶外活動，網球、高爾夫球、板球、橄欖球、足球等運動都很風行；澳洲人也熱愛水上運動，因為大多數人都住在近海的地方，游泳、衝浪、潛水、釣魚都十分普遍，到海邊玩，享受陽光也很常見。澳洲中部、西部、北部大部分的地方都野趣十足，是觀賞野生動植物的好去處，除了春天可以欣賞繁花開滿沙漠，一整年也都看得到袋鼠、無尾熊、鱷魚等動物，以及數百種五彩繽紛的鳥兒。

　　澳洲這個國家，是觀光的絕佳去處，各種景觀豐富多樣，加上面積廣大，人口又稀少，總有地方可以享受獨自一人的歡樂，全年無時無刻都適合前往，但有一點別忘了，就是愈往北走，天氣反而愈熱。

Kangaroo

袋鼠中只有母袋鼠才有育嬰袋；袋鼠是十分奇特的動物，可以一次交配多次受精，母袋鼠沒有胎盤，懷孕期很短，約一個月小袋鼠即可出生。

剛出生的小袋鼠只有3公分大，會順著母袋鼠為牠整理好的毛路爬至育嬰袋，育嬰袋中有乳房可提供小袋鼠乳汁，小袋鼠便在育嬰袋中成長，待三、四個月後會探頭出來看外面的世界，也會跑出來玩；約八個月，就完全離開袋子，不過這時的小袋鼠並未完全斷奶，偶爾還會探頭入育嬰袋內吃奶。

koala

無尾熊也有人稱之為樹熊，但實際上牠不是熊類。無尾熊是屬於有袋類的動物，牠們剛出生時還沒有發展完成，而是在熊媽媽的袋中繼續生長。而袋熊(wombat)可以說是無尾熊的遠親，他們兩者的「袋子」都是位於後方；而大部份有袋動物的袋子都是位在前面的，像是袋鼠、負鼠(possum)等等。無尾熊目前只在澳洲東方的海岸處有發現。

無尾熊不吃尤加利樹以外的葉子。而且在約六百種的尤加利樹裡，只挑約三十五種來吃。無尾熊吃尤加利葉的時候，是一片一片地邊聞香味邊吃。無尾熊身上的毛不會吸收雨水，因此不會被雨水淋濕而感到寒冷。在下雨天，無尾熊總是捲著身體，靜靜等待雨停。

5 *Triathlon*

Where there is a will, there is a way.

Triathlon

What was the most challenging physical exercise you have ever faced? Perhaps it was running a long distance or climbing a mountain. Whatever it was, you will probably remember how drained and exhausted you were at the end of it and how sore your muscles felt the next day. But how you felt then can not compare with how the people must feel while competing in the 5 world's most difficult sporting event, the ultimate test of fitness and endurance known as the triathlon.

The triathlon became well-known in the 1980's and has remained popular ever since. Each race consists of three stages: the swim, the bicycle ride and the run. The distances covered by each stage of the triathlon differ 10 from race to race, but the order of swim, ride and run always remains the same. Professional triathletes can expect to face a three kilometer swim, a one hundred and eighty kilometer bicycle ride and a forty-two kilometer run. A race like this will take professionals about nine hours to complete. The most famous triathlon is held every October in Hawaii and attracts competitors 15 from all over the world. But not all the competitors actually complete the event because exhaustion claims many victims.

Triathletes are dedicated athletes with busy training schedules. Everything they do for months is focused to ensure they are at the peak of their fitness on the day of their race. Because a triathlon is such a demanding 20 event, the human body can only endure two or three races per year and about twelve to fifteen in a lifetime. This makes triathlon a highly specialized and unique sport.

A triathlon can be raced in two ways. In the team triathlon, three team members concentrate on one event each. The most popular and prestigious is 25 the solo triathlon, where one man or woman completes all three stages by him or herself. Each professional triathlon attracts major sponsorships, prize money and a large television audience. Everyone wants to know about the most grueling sporting event in existence.

For most people, a triathlon sounds like an impossible event. Obviously   30
it is impossible to compete with the top athletes in a triathlon like the one
held in Hawaii. But actually a triathlon is a great test of all-around fitness and
the distances can be modified to be more realistic for the rest of us. For
example, there are schools, sports clubs and universities that organize their
own triathlons. In these events, the swim might be five hundred meters, the   35
bicycle ride twenty kilometers and the run five kilometers.

It is easy to organize a triathlon among your friends because the only
equipment a triathlon requires is a bicycle for each competitor. And
organizing your own event gives you the freedom to choose the distances you
must cover in each stage. If you are someone who prides yourself on your   40
fitness, then perhaps you can join a group of people and start training for a
triathlon. It would be nice to know you have faced and completed the ultimate
physical challenge.

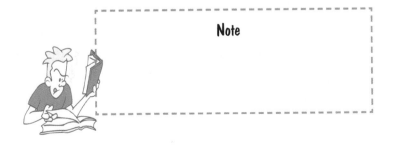

Note

Multiple Choice

—— 1. It is common for people to have sore muscles ——————.

   (A) when they are exhausted due to lack of sleep or lack of fitness

   (B) if they are well prepared for a race

   (C) if they stand too long under the sun

   (D) after they have faced a grueling physical challenge

—— 2. Every triathlon must ——————.

   (A) be only for professional triathletes who are in peak physical condition

   (B) consist of three events that can be completed in any order

   (C) be completed in the same order, otherwise it is not a real triathlon

   (D) be held in Hawaii because there has the only perfect place for such a sporting event

—— 3. The three stages of triathlon in the order are ——————.

   (A) the swim, the run and the bicycle ride

   (B) the swim, the car race and the bicycle ride

   (C) the swim, the bicycle ride and the run

   (D) the run, the swim and the bicycle ride

—— 4. Each year, the triathlon in Hawaii ——————.

   (A) claims many victims of exhaustion who cannot finish the event

   (B) is held among friends and shown around the world on live television

   (C) takes more than one day to complete because of the long solo stages

   (D) is held in July

—— 5. A professional triathlete ——————.

   (A) is a dedicated athlete with busy training schedules

   (B) often fails to complete a triathlon because of the exhaustion

   (C) can endure seven or eight races per year and about thirty in the lifetime

   (D) will die earlier than common people

—— 6. A unique feature of the professional triathlon is —————.
  (A) that it can only be completed less than twenty times because it is so hard
  (B) that it attracts major sponsorships and prize money because of its difficulty
  (C) the type of person who watches people suffer exhaustion on television
  (D) the one hundred and eighty kilometer ride

—— 7. A triathlon can be raced —————.
  (A) wherever there are teams of people who want to enter a solo event
  (B) on a team basis for three people or on a solo basis for one person
  (C) anywhere as long as there is a large enough television audience
  (D) only on a solo basis for one person, which makes it more exciting

—— 8. It is possible to modify a triathlon —————.
  (A) so that each race doesn't take nine hours to complete
  (B) but impossible to have a triathlon where competitors complete only one stage
  (C) but this is not recommended to triathlons held in school
  (D) so that a triathlete can endure more than fifty races in the lifetime

—— 9. Each competitor in a triathlon —————.
  (A) will need a bicycle if he or she is competing in the team event
  (B) will need to choose their own distances depending on their fitness level
  (C) will always require a bicycle if he or she is competing in the solo event
  (D) will compete both in the solo and team event to show his or her great strength

—— 10. The distances covered in each stage of a triathlon —————.
  (A) must not change between schools and sports clubs
  (B) should be long enough to ensure that the competitors fail to finish
  (C) should be the same
  (D) may be decided by the event organizers and competitors

Try This!

The following sentences are the explanations of certain words. Please match the words with the right sentences.

legs	competitor	draining	triathlon
	concentrate	modify	stages

1) a kind of sport consist of the swim, the bicycle ride, and the run
_____

2) to give all your attention to something _____

3) to change something _____

4) a person who takes part in races _____

5) a word, same as "exhausting" _____

6) swim, run, and bicycle ride are three _____ in a triathlon

7) the long parts of your body that become sore after running _____

Key Words

all-around *adj.* 全盤的

challenging *adj.* 挑戰性的

compete *v.* 競爭

competitor *n.* 競爭者

concentrate *v.* 專心

dedicated *adj.* 專注的

demanding *adj.* 苛求的

differ *v.* 相異

drain *v.* 枯竭

endurance *n.* 耐力

equipment *n.* 設備

exhausted *adj.* 疲憊的

exhaustion *n.* 竭盡

existence *n.* 存在

fitness *n.* 健康

focus *v.* 專注

grueling *adj.* 激烈的

Hawaii 夏威夷

modify *v.* 調節

muscle *n.* 肌肉

obviously *adv.* 顯然地

peak *n.* 尖峰

physical *adj.* 身體的

prestigious *adj.* 聲望高的

pride *v.* 自豪

professional *adj.* 專業的

realistic *adj.* 實際的

solo *adj.* 單獨的

sore *adj.* 痠痛的

sponsorship *n.* 贊助

stage *n.* 階段

triathlete *n.* 三項鐵人

triathlon *n.* 鐵人三項比賽

ultimate *adj.* 終極的

unique *adj.* 獨特的

victim *n.* 受害者

鐵人三項

你碰過最有挑戰性的體能運動是什麼？也許是長跑，也許是爬山，但不管是什麼，你可能還記得，結束時全身筋疲力竭，第二天肌肉也痠得不得了，可是不管當時你覺得多累，程度都比不上世界上難度最高的運動的參賽者，這種體能和耐力的終極試煉，就是鐵人三項。

1980年代，鐵人三項變得有名起來，之後就風行不輟。每次比賽包含三個階段：游泳、自行車和跑步，鐵人三項每一階段的距離因比賽而異，不過游泳、自行車、跑步的順序是不變的，鐵人三項的職業選手面對的很可能是三公里的游泳、一百八十公里的自行車和四十二公里的長跑，這樣的比賽，職業選手要九個小時左右才能完成。每年十月在夏威夷舉行的鐵人三項最負盛名，吸引世界各地好手前來角逐，但不是每位參賽者都能完成整個賽程，因為很多人到最後都體力不支。

鐵人三項的選手都是專注認真的運動員，訓練行程排得很滿，一連好幾個月的所作所為只有一個目的，就是要確保他們能在比賽當天處於體能的高峰。由於鐵人三項是一種要求很嚴苛的賽事，人的身體一年只能承受兩、三次的比賽，一生中大約只能負荷十二到十五次的比賽，這也使得鐵人三項成為非常專門而且相當特殊的運動。

鐵人三項有兩種比賽方式，一種是鐵人三項團體賽，由三名隊員專注各自的一項比賽，不過最風行也最負盛名的還是鐵人三項的個人賽，由一名男性或女性獨力完成三個階段。鐵人三項的職業賽能吸引相當大的贊助，也有高額的獎金，以及廣大的電視觀眾，大家對於現行最耗費體力的運動比賽，都想一探究竟。

　　對很多人來說，鐵人三項聽起來就好像不可能的任務，很明顯的，要和頂尖的運動員在像是夏威夷舉辦的鐵人三項比賽中一較高下是不可能的。不過鐵人三項其實是測驗全面體能最好的方法，至於我們一般人比賽的距離，可以調整得比較實際一點。舉例來說，不少學校、運動俱樂部、大學都會籌辦自己的鐵人三項比賽，這些賽事可能是游泳五百公尺，自行車二十公里，跑步五公里。

　　要安排朋友之間的鐵人三項很簡單，因為鐵人三項中唯一需要的裝備，就是每位參賽者需有一部腳踏車，而且舉辦自己的比賽，讓你們有自由選擇每一個階段所需的距離。假如你對自己的體能很自豪，不妨和一群人著手進行鐵人三項的訓練，勇敢面對這種終極的體能挑戰而且比完全程，這將會是一種絕佳的體驗。

Unit 6

"Twist and Shout"

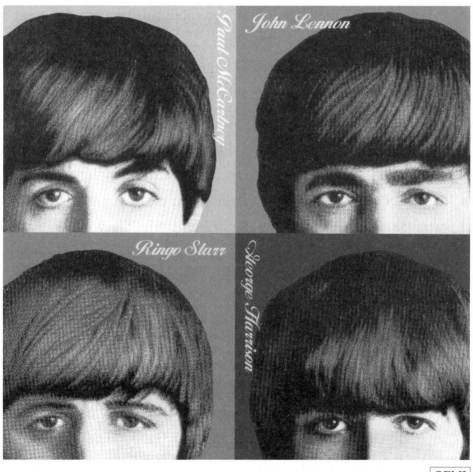

Paul McCartney

John Lennon

Ringo Starr

George Harrison

©EMI

When live in the world of grief,
There will be an answer.
Let it be...

"Twist and Shout"

In the 1960's, four young men from the working class city of Liverpool invented a new sound in pop music. Soon after, teenagers throughout England and the rest of the world heard this sound played over and over again on their radios and in their dance halls. The popularity of the music spread quickly, and with it came huge record sales and concerts full of screaming fans. The 5 music world had never seen such an enormous impact made by one band. The band was called "The Beatles" and they were about to become the greatest pop music band in history.

The Beatles were actually normal young men from working class families. What made them standout was that they were all brilliant musicians. 10 John Lennon played the guitar, Paul McCartney played the bass guitar, George Harrison played the lead guitar and Ringo Starr played the drums. All four members of the band sang although most of the singing was shared between John and Paul. They all wore fashionable clothes, grew thick black hair and portrayed an image to the public of being friendly young men. But 15 when it came to music, there was no other band that could match their songs and success. By 1964, John, Paul, George and Ringo were the most famous entertainers in the world. Everywhere they went, they were followed by thousands of screaming fans. It was a phenomenon that became known as "Beatlemania." 20

Early Beatles songs had popular melodies and lyrics that were mostly about love. Many of these songs became instant hits such as "Twist and Shout," "Love Me Do" and "I Want to Hold Your Hand." The Beatles were also the first English band to have major success in the United States. In April 1964, the Beatles held the top five spots on the American charts and had 25 twelve songs in the top one hundred. No band before or after the Beatles has come close to matching this success. As the band progressed through the sixties, their style became more experimental and artistic. Yet despite this

change, their music remained the most popular and influential in the world. Songs like "Hey Jude," "All You Need is Love" and "Yesterday" are typical   30
of their later style.

Between 1962 and 1970, the Beatles released ten records. They also released many songs as singles and made three movies. In fact, the Beatles were so popular and famous that they became the number one symbol of the sixties for many people. These days Beatles music is still popular with young   35
people. Many songs by the Beatles are just as well known today as they were when they first came out. The image of John, Paul, George and Ringo remains clear in the minds of most people and their pictures can often be seen in music stores and magazines. Their music was so innovative and influential that the Beatles style can often be heard in many kinds of modern pop music   40
today. Quite simply, the Beatles were the greatest pop music band ever.

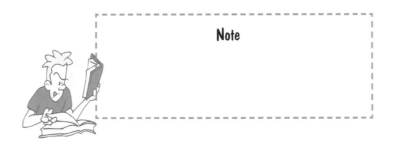

Note

True or False

——(1) The Beatles were four young men from wealthy families of Liverpool.

——(2) The Beatles invented a sound that was new to pop music.

——(3) The Beatles became known as the greatest band in history because no other band made so many records.

——(4) Many people liked the Beatles because of their music and also because of their image.

——(5) The Beatles used to wear fashionable clothes and grow thick black hair.

——(6) John and Paul did most of the singing but sometimes George and Ringo sang as well.

——(7) The early Beatles songs were more popular than the later Beatles songs because more people wanted to hear love songs.

——(8) The Beatles' record of holding the top five songs on the American charts has never been repeated.

——(9) When the Beatles finished in 1970, people stopped listening to their music.

——(10) The Beatles were so good that they still have an influence over pop bands today.

Try This!

Fact and Fiction.
For the following statements, circle the facts and cross out the fiction.

The Beatles

John, Paul, George and Ringo   thick black hair

fashionable musicians and hairdressers

young men from working class backgrounds   innovative

created the ''Beatlemania'' phenomenon

world-famous in the 1960's   famous for their music and painting

no longer popular   screaming fans

kept making the same style of music

greater chart success in the USA than any other band

Key Words

artistic *adj.* 藝術的	experimental *adj.* 實驗的	phenomenon *n.* 現象
band *n.* 樂團	fashionable *adj.* 新潮的	pop *adj.* 流行的
bass *adj.* 低音的	hit *n.* 成功	portray *v.* 扮演
Beatlemania *n.* 披頭熱潮	impact *n.* 影響	progress *v.* 進展
brilliant *adj.* 聰穎的	influential *adj.* 有影響的	record *n.* 唱片
chart *n.* 圖表	innovative *adj.* 創新的	release *v.* 發行
despite *prep.* 儘管	lead *v.* 主導	scream *v.* 尖叫
drum *n.* 鼓	lyrics *n.* 歌詞	standout *adj.* 卓越的
entertainer *n.* 演藝人員	melody *n.* 旋律	twist *v.* 扭曲

"Twist and Shout"

（註：此標題為披頭四所發行的一首歌曲）

　　1960年代，四個年輕人來自勞工階級為主的利物浦市，他們在流行音樂中創造出全新的聲音，不久之後，英國各地以及全世界其餘各國的青少年，不管是聽廣播或是到舞廳，反覆聽到的都是這種新的樂聲。這種音樂很快就大受歡迎，緊接著就是唱片大賣，演唱會滿是尖叫的歌迷。音樂界之前從沒見過哪個樂團有這麼大的影響力，而這個樂團就是「披頭四」，他們當時很快就成為史上最偉大的流行樂團。

　　披頭四其實是四個普通的年輕人，都來自勞工階級的家庭，他們之所以能嶄露頭角，是因為他們都是才華洋溢的音樂家，吉他手是約翰藍儂，低音吉他手是保羅麥卡尼，主吉他手是喬治哈里遜，鼓手是林哥史達，四個樂團成員都有演唱，不過主唱還是由約翰與保羅兩人擔任。他們個個衣著新潮，一頭又黑又厚的頭髮，而且在公眾面前塑造一種新好青年的形象，但是說到音樂，其他樂團的歌曲和成就都望塵莫及。1964年，約翰、保羅、喬治、林哥四個人已經是全世界最出名的演藝人員，不管走到哪裡，無數瘋狂的歌迷緊追在後，這種現象就是「披頭熱潮」。

　　披頭四早期的歌曲都有琅琅上口的旋律，而歌詞也以愛情為主，這些歌大多立刻就大賣，像是"Twist and Shout"、"Love Me Do"、"I Want to Hold Your Hand"等歌曲。披頭四也是頭一個在美國高度成功的英國樂團，1964年四月，披頭四占據全美排行榜的前五名，而且前一百名中，披頭四的歌曲更有十二首之多。披頭四的成就可說是空前絕後，從沒有過其他樂團能夠相抗衡，六○年代隨著樂團的漸次發展，他們的風格也變得更富實驗性與藝術性，不過儘管有這種改變，他們的音樂依然獨步全球，風靡程度與影響力無人能及。一些歌曲，像是"Hey Jude"、"All You Need is Love"、"Yesterday"都是他們後期典型的風格。

　　1962年到1970年間，披頭四一共發行了十張唱片，他們也發行了不少的單曲，演了三部電影，其實六〇年代披頭四紅得不得了，不僅家喻戶曉，更是許多人最愛的偶像。直到最近，披頭四的音樂還是很受年輕人喜愛，很多披頭四演唱的歌曲到了今天，還是跟當年剛推出時一樣廣為人知，約翰、保羅、喬治、林哥的形象在很多人的心目中鮮明依舊，而他們的照片在唱片行以及雜誌上都還看得到，他們的音樂十分創新，又極富影響力，所以時下許多新潮的流行音樂中，還聽得到披頭四風格，無怪乎披頭四的創作是有史以來最了不起的流行音樂。

Yellow Submarine

In the town where I was born
Lived a man who sailed to sea
And he told us of his life
In the land of submarines

So we sailed up to the sun
Till we found the sea of green
And we lived beneath the waves
In our yellow submarine

* We all live in our yellow submarine,
Yellow submarine, yellow submarine
We all live in our yellow submarine,
Yellow submarine, yellow submarine

And our friends are all on board
Many more of them live next door
And the band begins to play

As we live a life of ease
Everyone of us has all we need
Sky of blue and sea of green
In our yellow submarine.

Unit 7

Making Movies

This world is a comedy to those that think,
a tragedy to those that feel.

Making Movies

Movies can be made from any story. Using special effects, interesting locations, and talented actors, movie makers take people into a world where anything becomes possible. Some of the most popular movie genres include: action, drama, science fiction, comedy, historical, horror and documentary. But when you are watching a movie, have you ever thought about the work   5
that must go into its production?

The most popular movies in the world are made in Hollywood, California. In Hollywood, the movie industry is dominated by large production companies such as Paramount, Universal, Fox, Columbia and Metro Golden Meyer. Hollywood movies have budgets of millions of US   10
dollars. This money is needed to pay for the best available special effects, actors and actresses, directors, producers, and many supporting workers who work on the technical aspects of movie making.

The person responsible for artistic matters, such as acting and filming is called the director. As movies are mostly known for their artistic and creative   15
achievements, it is the directors that become famous when movies are successful. In modern times, some of the best known directors from Hollywood are Steven Spielberg, Robert Altman, Oliver Stone and Quentin Tarentino. In particular, Steven Spielberg has become famous as the director genius of Hollywood. His movies are known to combine emotion and   20
incredible special effects. You may have seen some of his movies such as "Jurassic Park," "E.T.," "Schindler's List" and "Saving Private Ryan."

Movie making usually occurs in the following order. The story and its dialog are described in the script. Usually the script is based on a book but sometimes the script is written directly for the movie. When the script is   25
ready, the director takes the cameramen and goes scouting. This means searching for locations that match the scenes in the script. When the locations don't exist in reality, they may have to be built in a studio. The next step,

called casting, is to try and find the right actors and actresses.

Most of the organization of movie making is done by the producer. He 30 or she is responsible for having all the necessary parts assembled at the right place at the right time. The actual filming of movies is usually done as fast as possible because the costs of having so many people on location are very high. People involved in movie making generally agree that filming is by far the most difficult and frustrating part of making movies. Finally, the movie is 35 ready for editing. This is when the special effects, stunt scenes, refinement of photography and sound are added.

Although Hollywood makes the most famous movies, there are also successful movies made in other countries with much smaller budgets. Often these movies are just as powerful as Hollywood movies, even though they 40 don't have the same special effects and famous actors. These movies often rely more heavily on clever plots, artistic beauty and complex characters to captivate their audience. If you watch many movies, you will understand that it takes more than just money to make a great movie.

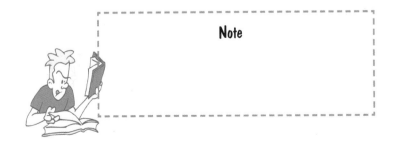

Note

True or False

——(1) Movie makers can turn any story into a movie using special effects, interesting locations and talented actors.

——(2) Hollywood movies are the most popular in the world because they have huge budgets to spend on the best available movie makers.

——(3) Both the producer and the director make important artistic decisions.

——(4) Directors often become the most famous people involved in making movies because they make the biggest decisions.

——(5) Movies can be made in different ways because each movie is unlike any other.

——(6) The director should always assemble all the necessary parts at the right place at the right time because the costs of having so many people on location are very high.

——(7) Scouting occurs when the director and cameramen start filming in a studio.

——(8) Editing is normally the last part of movie making because it occurs once the filming is finished.

——(9) Non-Hollywood movies are always better than Hollywood movies because they have better stories.

——(10) "Jurassic Park," "E.T.," and "Saving Private Ryan" are great non-Hollywood movies.

Try This!

You are the director of a new science fiction film. Consider the following stages of film making and place them in the correct order by writing a number beside each stage.

———— build the backgrounds in the studio

———— transform the book into a script

———— edit and refine the film

———— help the actors prepare for their roles

———— show the script to a production company and receive funding for the film

———— attend the premier screening and talk to the media about the film

———— find a good story from a science fiction book

———— search for locations to film with some of your new production crew

———— film the movie

Key Words

achievement *n.* 成就	documentary *n.* 記錄片	involve *v.* 牽涉
assemble *v.* 聚集	dominate *v.* 支配	location *n.* 地點
budget *n.* 預算	drama *n.* 戲劇	plot *n.* 情節
cameraman *n.* 攝影師	editing *v.* 剪接	producer *n.* 製片
captivate *v.* 使著迷	effect *n.* 效果	refinement *n.* 精煉
cast *v.* 派定演員	fiction *n.* 小說	scene *n.* 場景
combine *v.* 結合	film *v.* 拍攝	scout *v.* 偵察
comedy *n.* 喜劇	frustrate *v.* 使受挫	script *n.* 劇本
complex *adj.* 複雜的	genre *n.* 類	studio *n.* 攝影棚
dialog *n.* 對話	horror *n.* 恐怖	stunt *n.* 特技

電影製作

　　什麼故事都能拍成電影，只要運用特效、吸引人的外景，再加上有天賦的演員，電影製作者就可以把觀眾帶進一個一切都能成真的世界，幾種大家最愛看的電影類型包括動作片、劇情片、科幻片、喜劇片、史料片、驚悚片、記錄片等，可是看電影時，你可曾想過電影的製作過程要付出什麼心血嗎？

　　世界上最受歡迎的電影是在加州好萊塢拍攝的，好萊塢的電影業是由一些大型的製片公司所主導，像是派拉蒙、環球、福斯、哥倫比亞、米高梅等公司，好萊塢電影的預算動輒數百萬美元，這筆錢的確有其必要，如此才能做出最棒的特效，也才請得起最好的男女演員、導演、製片以及許許多多處理製片技術的幕後工作人員。

　　拍一部電影，負責像是動作和拍片等藝術部分的人叫做導演，由於一部出色的電影，好就好在它的藝術和創意方面的成就，所以電影拍得成功，最出名的自然就是導演了。現在好萊塢最有名的導演就屬史蒂芬史匹柏、勞勃阿特曼、奧利佛史東、昆汀泰倫提諾等人，特別是史蒂芬史匹柏是好萊塢出了名的天才導演，他的電影以結合情感和驚人的特效聞名，你可能也已看過幾部他導的電影，像是「侏羅紀公園」、「外星人」、「辛德勒的名單」還有「搶救雷恩大兵」。

　　電影製作通常有下列順序，首先要有描述劇情和對話的劇本，通常劇本是以一本書為底本，不過有時候劇本是針對電影寫的；有了劇本以後，導演就要帶著攝影師去勘景，也就是去找適合劇本場景的外景，如果現實中沒有這樣的外景存在，就得在攝影場地搭造布景；再下一步就是挑選演員，挖掘合適的男女演員。

　　電影製作大部分的大小事安排都是製片的工作，什麼時候應該在什麼地方做什麼事，都是製片一手包辦，電影的實際拍攝通常力求速戰速決，因為要雇用這麼多人到場，成本很高。參與過電影錄製的人一般都會同意，拍一部電影最困難也最讓人灰心的，往往就是錄製電影的這段期間。最後到了電影剪輯的階段，這時候會加入特效、特技場面、修片以及音效。

　　縱使好萊塢拍的電影十分出名，還是有人在其他國家只用了一小筆的預算，就拍了相當出色的電影，就算這些電影沒有相同的特效，也沒有知名的演員，還是一樣能震撼人心，不輸好萊塢電影。這些電影通常倚仗的是更巧妙的情節、藝術性更高的美感，還有多樣的角色，藉此贏得觀眾的青睞，假如你看過很多的電影，你就會了解，要拍出一部好電影，光用錢是不夠的。

Unit 8

Earthquakes

地震震垮了房屋，
卻震不垮我們的信心！

Earthquakes

Every year, approximately one million earthquakes occur around the world. Most earthquakes have no effect on people because they happen so far under the oceans that their shock waves don't reach land. But when they occur below populated areas such as towns and cities, the devastation can be severe. When the earth starts shaking, buildings may collapse and landslides   5
may destroy everything in their path. Another danger during an earthquake comes from fires which can easily break out in many places at once after gas pipes burst. And if fires break out all over a city, then they may become too much for firefighters to control.

Earthquakes are caused by friction between moving sections of the   10
earth. These sections, also called plates, are constantly moving. As the plates collide, they sometimes break due to enormous pressure. When this break happens, huge shock waves generate outwards. If the shock waves are very powerful, they will reach the surface of the earth and cause it to vibrate.

Over many years, scientists have measured the location, size and   15
frequency of earthquakes. This information gives us a clear picture of where the major fault lines are located around the world. The fault line that lies across California is called the San Andreas Fault. The amazing thing about this fault is that it actually occurs on the surface of the earth and can be seen by people. The last major earthquake on the San Andreas Fault happened in   20
1906. Because that earthquake occurred a hundred years ago, experts say there must now be a lot of pressure built up in California that will be released with the next earthquake. In fact, experts often predict that in the near future the San Andreas Fault will cause a massive earthquake that could possibly devastate San Francisco or Los Angeles.   25

Turkey is another country which has suffered from earthquakes. In recent years, a series of earthquakes occurred measuring as high as 7.2 on the Richter scale, causing enormous damage in the northern part of the country.

Over fifteen thousand people died in these earthquakes, mainly by being in apartment blocks that collapsed as the ground shook. In 1923, a severe   30
earthquake occurred under the city of Yokohama, Japan. When this earthquake occurred, thousands of people were crushed by buildings, however the fires that immediately followed the Yokohama earthquake caused the greatest damage. In Yokohama, ninety-five percent of the city buildings were burnt down, killing approximately one hundred thousand   35
people. At the same time, fires broke out fifty kilometers away in the city of Tokyo. A further eighty thousand people were burnt to death in Tokyo, making this earthquake the most deadly in modern times.

Most earthquakes occur along fault lines, but it is also possible for them to happen anywhere in the world. During an earthquake you should try to get   40
under a door frame or a table if you are caught inside. Also remember it is much better to get outside, away from buildings and objects that may crash to the ground. Nobody knows when an earthquake will occur, so it is vital to know what to do when the earth starts to shake.

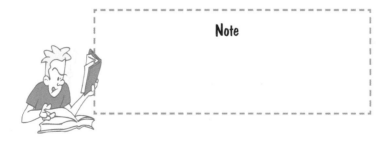

Note

True or False

——(1) Most earthquakes aren't felt by people because they mostly occur where people don't live.

——(2) Earthquakes are caused by friction between moving sections of the earth.

——(3) Shock waves make the ground vibrate and cause damage to buildings.

——(4) Scientists measure earthquakes just to find out when the next earthquake will occur.

——(5) The San Andreas Fault in California will one day devastate Los Angeles or San Francisco because it can be seen on the surface of the earth.

——(6) The recent Turkish earthquakes killed the most people in modern times.

——(7) Most of the people who died in the Japanese earthquake of 1923 were crushed by buildings in both Yokohama and Tokyo.

——(8) Besides along fault lines, it is possible that earthquakes happen anywhere in the world.

——(9) Everyone should know what to do if the earth starts to shake.

——(10) If you are not outside during an earthquake, you will certainly die.

Try This!

Find a word in the box that fits with each set of words.

day	frame	letter	hard	post	line
station	fire	top	home	library	lock

_____ fighter · brigade · engine   train · fault · air _____

_____ card · graduate · office   mountain · desk · roof _____

_____ made · less · town   door · picture · window _____

_____ bag · brake · book   _____ break · dream · time

Key Words

approximately *adv.* 大約	fault *n.* 斷層	populate *v.* 居住於
block *n.* 石塊	frame *n.* 框架	predict *v.* 預測
burst *v.* 爆炸	frequency *n.* 頻率	release *v.* 釋出
collapse *v.* 倒塌	friction *n.* 摩擦	Richter scale *n.* 芮氏地震儀
collide *v.* 碰撞	generate *v.* 產生	section *n.* 陸塊
crush *v.* 壓碎	landslide *n.* 山崩	severe *adj.* 猛烈的
deadly *adj.* 致命的	massive *adj.* 大量的	shock wave *n.* 震波
devastate *v.* 使荒廢	path *n.* 路徑	Turkey 土耳其
devastation *n.* 毀壞	pipe *n.* 管	vibrate *v.* 震動
earthquake *n.* 地震	plate *n.* 陸塊	vital *adj.* 極重要的

地震

　　全球每年發生的地震約有一百萬次，大部分的地震不會對人類造成影響，因為它們發生在海底下相當深的地方，所以震波無法到達陸地，不過一旦地震發生在人煙稠密處的地底，比方說城鎮或都市，那麼災情可能會很嚴重。大地只要開始搖動，建築物有可能會倒塌，而山崩也可能摧毀其行經路上的一切事物。地震期間另一項危害來源就是火災，瓦斯管破裂之後，很多地方很容易立刻就發生火警，而且萬一全市都發生大火，那很可能一發不可收拾，消防人員是無法控制得住的。

　　地震是由陸塊移動時產生的摩擦造成的，這些陸塊又稱做地殼，經常在移動，地殼相互碰撞的時候，偶爾會因壓力過大而斷裂，一旦發生斷裂，會產生強大的震波向外傳送，假如震波威力夠強大的話，就能達到地球表面，造成地表的振動。

　　多年來，科學家已經測量地震發生的位置、規模和頻率，這份資料很清楚顯示全世界主要的斷層帶位於何處，通過加州的斷層帶稱做聖安地列斯斷層，該斷層驚人之處在於它其實是裸露在地表看得到的地方，聖安地列斯斷層上一次發生大地震是在1906年，由於地震發生在一百年前，專家表示目前勢必累積了很多的能量，將在下一次地震時釋放，其實專家常常預言在不久的將來，聖安地列斯斷層會引發一場強烈的地震，有可能會摧毀舊金山或是洛杉磯。

　　土耳其是另一個為地震所苦的國家，近年來，芮氏地震規模最高達到七點二的地震接二連三發生，造成該國北部損失慘重，超過一萬五千人死於這些地震，主要是因為困在公寓的瓦礫堆中，而公寓是因地層搖動而倒塌的。1923年，日本橫濱市發生一次嚴重的地震，地震發生的時候，幾千名的居民遭到房屋壓傷，可是橫濱大地震之後，緊接著發生的火災卻造成最慘重的災害，橫濱市內百分之九十五的建築物付之一炬，奪走了十萬條左右的人命，同一期間，火苗也在五十公里外的東京市竄燒，又有八萬人在東京葬身火窟，導致這次地震是現代地震中傷亡最慘重的一次。

　　地震大多發生在斷層帶沿線，不過世界各地也都有可能發生地震，地震來臨時，若是困在屋內，應該躲在門框下方或是桌子底下，記得最好到戶外，遠離建築物以及可能砸下來的物體，沒有人知道地震什麼時候會發生，所以牢記大地開始搖動時應該怎麼辦是很重要的。

震度分級法

我國的震度級數原本共分七級(0-6級)，但是九二一大地震的震度已經遠超過原來的設定，因此在89年6月將震度分級改為八級，第七級的名稱為「劇震」。

震度分級		人的感受	屋內情形	屋外情形
0	無感	人無感覺		
1	微震	人靜止時可感覺微小搖晃。		
2	輕震	多數人可感到搖晃，睡眠中的人有部分會醒來。	電燈等懸掛物有小搖晃。	靜止的汽車輕輕搖晃，類似卡車經過，但歷時很短。
3	弱震	幾乎所有人都感覺到搖晃，有些人會有恐懼感。	房屋震動，碗盤門窗發出聲音，懸掛物搖擺。	靜止的汽車明顯搖動，電線略有搖晃。
4	中震	有相當程度的恐懼感，部分的人會尋求躲避之處，睡眠中的人幾乎都會驚醒。	房屋搖動甚烈，底座不穩物品傾倒，較重傢俱移動，可能有輕微災害。	汽車駕駛人略微有感，電線明顯搖晃，步行中的人也感到搖晃。
5	強震	大多數人會感到驚嚇恐慌。	部分牆壁產生裂痕，重傢俱可能翻倒。	部分牆壁產生裂痕，重傢俱可能翻倒。
6	烈震	搖晃劇烈以致站立困難。	部分建築物受損，重傢俱翻倒，門窗扭曲變形。	汽車駕駛人開車困難，出現噴沙噴泥現象。
7	劇震	搖晃劇烈以致無法依意志行動。	部分建築物受損嚴重或倒塌，幾乎所有傢俱都大幅移位或摔落地面。	山崩地裂，鐵軌彎曲，地下管線破壞。

資料來源：中央氣象局

Unit 9

The Ancient Egyptians

偉大又神秘的埃及王國…
金字塔下究竟隱藏了多少秘密？

The Ancient Egyptians

Egyptian culture arose approximately five thousand years ago near the Nile in North Eastern Africa. It was a unique culture that prospered for almost three thousand years, making it one of the longest lasting civilizations in history. Fortunately for people today, the Egyptians left many pieces of their art and writing in good condition. We can therefore piece together the way   5 these people lived and understand the ways in which they have influenced the modern world.

The Nile was very important for the ancient Egyptians. It provided rich soil for agriculture and an efficient means of transportation. Egyptian farmers began growing large quantities of food around the year 3000 B.C., and then   10 traveled down the Nile and into the Mediterranean Sea to trade. Once the people were easily fed, a society that became one of the most advanced in the world was formed. The Egyptians devised the 365 day calendar and were the first people to create a national government. They also invented a writing form by using pictures.   15

The ancient Egyptians were dark-skinned people with black hair. They mostly dressed in white linen garments and wore leather sandals on their feet. The Egyptians especially liked cosmetics and jewelry. Women wore red lip powder and colored their eyebrows with gray, black and green paint. Men also outlined their eyes and sometimes wore as much makeup as the women.   20 Both men and women wore perfume and jewelry such as rings, bracelets and necklaces. The Egyptians also had a fascination with religion and life after death. Much of their time was spent preparing for life after death and this was the major reason behind their most famous constructions, the Pyramids. The Pyramids were built as massive tombs for Egyptian rulers. Each Pyramid was   25 built over a burial chamber in order to protect the dead soul and keep it safe from the common people.

Most of the Pyramids were built around 4,500 years ago. When people in the modern age began to explore the tombs underneath the Pyramids, they found jewelry, clothes, art and weapons. The objects in the tomb were for the 30 ruler to take into the next life. The art included paintings, showing what life was like in Egyptian times. The jewelry was the work of highly skilled craftsmen and the clothes gave experts a clear insight into the dress style of ancient Egypt. Thirty dynasties rose and fell during the years of ancient Egypt. One of the most famous rulers was Tutenkharmen of the 20th dynasty. 35 He was the ruler around the year 1300 B.C. and encouraged both old and modern forms of Egyptian religion. Tutenkharmen was one of Egypt's strongest leaders, and the gold and other jewelry found in his tomb are among the finest treasures ever found.

Today many artifacts from ancient Egypt remain in good condition and 40 can be viewed by tourists. Most of the Pyramids are located just south of the modern Egyptian city of Cairo, and every year they attract thousands of visitors. Yet despite what we know about the Egyptians, we still have unanswered questions. Many of these questions shall remain mysteries lost forever in time. 45

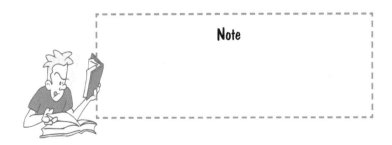

Note

Multiple Choice

—— 1. Egyptian culture arose ——————.

   (A) about one hundred years ago in South Western Africa

   (B) about one thousand years ago in South Eastern Africa

   (C) about five thousand years ago in North Eastern Asia

   (D) about five thousand years ago in North Eastern Africa

—— 2. We can study how Egyptian culture influenced modern western culture b y ——————.

   (A) looking at famous artifacts

   (B) understanding the Egyptian fascination with death

   (C) studying more about Egyptian history

   (D) figuring out how the Pyramids were built

—— 3. Once the Egyptians had enough food, they ——————.

   (A) had time to develop a strong culture

   (B) built huge pyramids all over Egypt

   (C) no longer wore jewelry

   (D) started to wear makeup

—— 4. The Egyptians made great advances ——————.

   (A) for their own time but did not influence our modern lives

   (B) during the thirty dynasties

   (C) so that modern tourists would be amazed

   (D) only in the dynasty of Tutenkharmen

—— 5. Egyptian men painted their faces ——————.

   (A) but Egyptian women only wore nice clothes

   (B) and wore jewelry

   (C) only when they prepared for death and life after death

   (D) but didn't wear any jewelry

—— 6. The Egyptian fascination with religion and life after death ————.

    (A) was a reason why the Pyramids were built

    (B) continues to confuse modern experts

    (C) did not influence other parts of Egyptian culture

    (D) made all the Egyptians today become superstitious

—— 7. We can tell what life was like in ancient Egypt because ————.

    (A) we now know everything about all thirty dynasties

    (B) many artifacts and constructions were left behind

    (C) the mysteries are no longer important

    (D) all the mysteries have been resolved by experts

—— 8. We know Tutenkharmen was an important ruler because ————.

    (A) his tomb contained many treasures

    (B) he wrote many books that we can still read

    (C) the 20th dynasty was by far the most influential

    (D) he planned to build all those large Pyramids

—— 9. Ancient Egyptian artifacts and the Pyramids ————.

    (A) can no longer be seen by tourists

    (B) are private collections belonging to rich people around the world

    (C) are all in perfect condition

    (D) are popular among modern tourists

—— 10. The capital of today's Egypt is ————.

    (A) the Nile

    (B) the Pyramids

    (C) Cairo

    (D) Egypt

Try This!

In the article about ancient Egyptians, there are many adjectives that describe nouns. Look at the following lists and match the correct adjectives and nouns by connecting them with a line.

Adjectives	Nouns
burial	people
dead	chamber
leather	tombs
black	soul
massive	sandals
ancient	soil
rich	world
modern	hair
common	Egyptians
lip	craftsman
skilled	powder

Key Words

ancient *adj.* 古代的	Egypt 埃及	Nile *n.* 尼羅河
arise *v.* 產生	Egyptian *n.* 埃及人	outline *v.* 畫輪廓
artifact *n.* 工藝品	eyebrow *n.* 眉毛	perfume *n.* 香水
bracelet *n.* 手環	fascination *n.* 著迷	piece *v.* 拼湊；*n.* 片
burial *n.* 墓地	feed *v.* 餵食	powder *n.* 粉末
Cairo 開羅	garment *n.* 服裝	prosper *v.* 昌盛
calendar *n.* 曆法	invent *v.* 創造	pyramid *n.* 金字塔
chamber *n.* 室	jewelry *n.* 珠寶	quantity *n.* 量
civilization *n.* 文明	leather *n.* 皮革	ring *n.* 戒指
construction *n.* 建築物	linen *n.* 亞麻布	sandal *n.* 便鞋
cosmetic *n.* 化妝品	lip *n.* 嘴唇	soil *n.* 土壤
craftsman *n.* 工匠	makeup *n.* 化妝	tomb *n.* 墓
devise *v.* 設計	mystery *n.* 謎	tourist *n.* 旅客
dynasty *n.* 朝代	necklace *n.* 項鍊	underneath *prep.* 在…之下

古埃及人

　　埃及文化大約在五千年前起源於非洲東北部的尼羅河流域，是一個發展興盛將近三千年的獨特文化，成為史上歷時最久的文化之一。今天的人很幸運，因為埃及人遺留了為數不少且保存完好的文物與史料，所以拼湊之後，我們就可以知道這些人的生活方式，也能了解埃及人對現今的世界有什麼影響。

　　尼羅河對古埃及人來說非常重要，不僅提供農業所需的肥沃土壤，也是方便快速的交通方式，西元前三千年左右，埃及農夫開始栽種大量的糧食，然後再沿尼羅河順流而下到地中海進行貿易。一旦人民得以酒足飯飽，一個社會體系就會接著形成，而埃及社會就成了世界上最開化的社會之一，埃及人設計了一套一年三百六十五天的曆法，也是第一個創制中央政府的民族，他們也發明了一種用圖畫表達的象形文字。

　　古埃及人是深色皮膚、黑色頭髮的民族，通常都穿白色的亞麻衣，腳上穿皮製的便鞋。埃及人特別喜好化妝品和珠寶，女人口塗紅色脂粉，眉毛也用灰、黑、綠等顏料加以上色；男人也會畫眼妝，有時化的妝也不比女人少，男人女人都會擦香水，也會佩帶珠寶，如戒指、手鐲、項鍊等。埃及人對於宗教和來世也很著迷，很多時間都用來替來世做準備，這也是他們最著名的建築物，也就是金字塔背後的主因。建造金字塔是要當作埃及國王的宏偉陵墓，每一座金字塔都建在墓室之上，是為了保護死者的靈魂不受一般人的打擾。

　　大部分金字塔建造的時間大約在四千五百年以前，現代人著手探究金字塔底下的墓室時，找到珠寶、衣物、藝術品、兵器等東西。這些墓中的器物是要給國王帶到來世的，藝術品包括一些圖畫，畫的是埃及時代的生活狀況；珠寶是技巧純熟的工匠所打造的作品，而衣服也讓專家看清楚古埃及時代的衣著風格。古埃及的悠悠歲月，三十個王朝的興衰起落，其中最著名的國王就是第二十王朝的圖騰卡門王，他是西元前一千三百年左右的國王，他不僅支持當時的宗教，也因而助長了埃及現代的宗教，圖騰卡門王是埃及眾多強勢領導者之一，在他墓中發現的金銀珠寶可說是目前的發現中最頂級的寶物。

　　時至今日，許多古埃及時代的工藝品依舊保存完好，可供遊客觀賞，大多數的金字塔就位在現今埃及開羅市的南方，每年吸引數以千計的觀光客，然而，儘管我們對埃及人有所了解，還是有疑點尚未獲得解答，許多問題至今依舊是個謎，將永遠消逝在時間的洪流中。

 最早養貓的民族

　　科學家相信，最早養貓的民族可能是埃及人。埃及人不但養貓養得早，甚至以貓為神，女神巴司特（Bast，或Bubastis）即為人身貓頭。不但如此，古埃及人如果打了貓，要受罰；殺了貓則需抵命。貓死了以後，常被製成木乃伊葬在貓塚裡，貓的墳墓中還有老鼠的木乃伊及一小碟牛奶，這類木乃伊現在已發現了不少。

Unit 10

Working Part-time

打工不僅能賺錢，還能學習獨立自主！
你想打什麼工呢？

Working Part-time

It's not easy being a student. You have to learn difficult information, take tests and do homework at night. When you are a student, you must organize your time to meet schedules, deadlines and examination timetables. And most of the time while you are a student, you have no money whatsoever. Well, actually the last part doesn't have to be true. You can 5 always get a part-time job.

These days, it's common for high school and university students to get a part-time job. Some students work in department stores or regular shops. Others work in cafés and restaurants, cooking food or serving customers. Some students work at supermarkets, stacking the shelves at night or 10 organizing the storage of food at the back of the supermarket when it comes from the warehouse. Students can also work part-time in factories and other production places. Like any other job, however, it is worth trying to get a part-time job that is interesting for you. For example, if you enjoy listening to music, then you could apply for a part-time job at all the CD stores in your 15 town. If you like movies, you could try and work part-time at a movie theater. If you like reading, you should consider working at a bookstore or library. By getting a part-time job at a place you find interesting, your performance at work will be better and you will enjoy your time more. Just because it's a part-time job doesn't mean it has to be boring. 20

The money you earn is an advantage of working part-time. But of course there are many other benefits as well. Every job you do will teach you new skills. Maybe you will learn how to cook new dishes or learn a faster way to clean. With many jobs in fast food restaurants and convenience stores, you will get practice at how to deal with customers. In other stores, you may have 25 to handle large amounts of cash and learn about stock control. By working part-time in an office, you will probably get to use computers in a way you haven't done before. Some students say they don't have time to work part-time. Perhaps this is true before exams. If so, it should be possible to ask your boss for time off around these crucial weeks. Another possibility for students 30 is to work during the holiday period. There's no doubt that getting a good job during the holidays will be looked on favorably by your future employers.

If you're having trouble getting motivated to work, then perhaps you should set yourself a reward. Maybe your reward could be a new CD player or a computer. Calculate how much money you need to save to buy yourself a 35 new asset such as this and calculate how long it will take to save that money. Before you know it, you will have bought what you wanted and discovered a new independence as well.

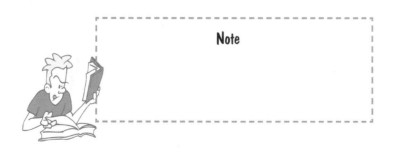

Note

True or False

——(1) Student life isn't difficult because there is always plenty of free time.

——(2) There are many reasons why students get part-time jobs, but there aren't many jobs they can choose from.

——(3) Part-time jobs are boring because they are never good jobs.

——(4) Students should try to get a part-time job that they find interesting.

——(5) If you like reading, you may have a part-time job in a restaurant where has a lot of menus for you to read.

——(6) If students don't have any work skills, they will probably not be able to get a part-time job.

——(7) Most students have enough time to work part-time if they can take time off before exams.

——(8) Holiday jobs have many advantages, including helping students get better jobs in the future.

——(9) A goal is a good idea because it gives the worker more motivation.

——(10) You can both earn money and own independence by doing a part-time job.

Try This!

Susan is so busy that she needs a timetable to help her get through the week. Read the following information and fill in the timetable gaps with the words: "Work," "Class," "Study," "Gym" and "Free."

	8 a.m.	10 a.m.	12 noon	2 p.m.	4 p.m.	6 p.m.	8 p.m.	10 p.m.
Monday								
Tuesday								
Wednesday								
Thursday								
Friday								

Susan's boss said,"I would like you to work on Monday, Wednesday and Friday nights from 6 p.m. until 10 p.m."

Susan's classes start at 8 a.m. and finish at 4 p.m., and her school timetable stays the same on Monday, Tuesday, Wednesday and Friday.

Examinations are held during class on the last day of the week.

"I like to go to the gym to relax after my examinations," said Susan.

The night before her weekly examinations, Susan always studies for four hours.

Susan says,"I like to keep Thursdays free, but I need to find two more hours in the week to study."

For three days of the week Susan is free after 4 p.m. when her classes finish.

Key Words

amount *n.* 數量	dish *n.* 菜餚	stack *v.* 堆起
asset *n.* 貴重物	favorably *adv.* 好意地	stock *n.* 存貨
benefit *n.* 益處	handle *v.* 處理	storage *n.* 儲藏
calculate *v.* 計算	motivate *v.* 引起動機	timetable *n.* 時間表
crucial *adj.* 重要的	performance *n.* 表現	warehouse *n.* 倉庫
deadline *n.* 最後期限	shelf *n.* 架子	whatsoever *pron.* 任何

打工

當學生並不簡單，得學習高深的學識、參加考試、晚上還要做功課，做學生的時候，必須安排時間，才能趕上課程進度、準時交作業、應付密密麻麻的考試時間表，而且學生大部分的時候都沒有什麼錢，嗯，也不一定是這樣，起碼你可以找一個兼職的工作。

最近高中生、大學生打工的情形很普遍，有些學生在百貨公司或是一般的店家工作；有些到咖啡店、餐廳打工，烹調食物或是替客人服務；也有人到超市工作，晚上把貨品上架，或是食物的存貨從倉庫運來時，在超市的後頭加以整理排放。學生也可以到工廠及其他的生產場所去打工，無論如何，就像其他的工作一樣，不管是什麼樣的兼職工作，只要你覺得有趣都值得一試。比方說，假如你喜歡聽音樂，那你可以到住家附近的CD唱片行應徵一份兼職的工作；假如你喜歡電影，你可以試試看到電影院打工；如果你喜歡看書，你可以考慮到書店或是圖書館工作。到一個你認為很有趣的地方去工作，你的工作表現一定會更加優異，而且你也會更快活，並不是說打工就一定得是很無趣的。

賺錢是打工的一項好處，可是當然還有其他的好處，每做一種工作就可以學到新的技巧，也許你會學到一些新菜餚的作法，或是學到怎樣打掃速度會比較快；而速食店和便利商店很多的工作都可以訓練你該如何和顧客應對；在其他的店舖，你也許得處理大筆的現金，也學得到倉儲管理；到辦公室打工，你可能會使用電腦，學到以前沒用過的方法。有些學生說他們沒有時間打工，在大考之前也許真是如此，這樣的話，應該可以要求上司在這幾個緊要的禮拜讓你放個假；還有另一種可能性，就是學生可以在假期當中工作，在假日找一份不錯的差事一定會讓你以後的雇主有一個好印象。

要是你提不起勁去工作的話，那麼你應該給自己設定獎賞，也許你可以犒賞自己一臺新的雷射音響或是一臺新電腦,算一下要存多少錢才能自己買下這一些東西,再算一算要存多久才行,你可能在不知不覺中就有能力買下你想要的東西,還發現自己多了一份獨立自主。

餐廳打工甘苦談

在學生生活中,除了課業及社團之外,佔據我大部分的時間就是打工囉!在因緣際會下,我到一家複合式餐飲店打工。何謂複合式餐飲呢?就是有賣餐點、咖啡、軟性飲料及調酒!

一開始我只是一個直接面對客人的外場工讀生…可別小看外場工讀生,他可是店裡最先面對客人的第一線喔,所以外場工讀生該注意哪些事項呢?

1. 面帶微笑:你的微笑可是會讓客人對這家店產生好印象,所以ㄚ…可別吝惜露出你甜美的笑容!客人會因此愛上這家店喔!

2. 細心:當外場工讀生可是培養你細心的最佳時機!客人的點餐、餐點要送至何處,可都是需要你的細心才能順利達成任務!

3. 耐心:在服務業的職場裡工作,難免會面對各式各樣的人,每個人的要求都不同,針對不同的需求給予不同及適宜的服務可是一門大學問…所以耐心是不可或缺的!

4. 服務為本,客人至上:何謂服務業呢?就是服務大眾。所以當你在工作時,你就必須本著服務的精神來服務客人,以達到客人的需求。其實大部分的客人都滿和氣、客氣的,只是有時候你就是會不小心遇到「傲客」,這時你當然不能當面不爽…你只能暗坎在心中,繼續以微笑面對客人。只要不發脾氣,我們是站的住腳的!

No pains, no gains!

11 **Dear Jane Sanders**

風呀，
可不可以請你吹走我的無助？

Dear Jane Sanders

If you're having personal problems and don't know who to turn to, then write a letter to Jane Sanders, the newspaper expert in matters of the heart.

Dear Jane Sanders,

I'm a twenty-year-old university student. I began going out with a guy four years ago who was one year older than I am. Throughout our last years of high school, we became very close and we both felt we were in love. One of the reasons I loved Peter was because of his enthusiasm and interest towards everything in the world. Therefore, I wasn't surprised when he told me about his plan to study in the United Kingdom for one year. Of course I didn't want him to leave but I knew his mind was set on the plan and we both knew how good the experience would be for his job prospects. When he left, we promised to write email most days and letters about important things. We also decided to call each other on the telephone occasionally. At the start, our communication worked exactly as planned. But gradually everything changed, and it was I who sent most of the emails and made most of the calls. Then just before he was due to return, he sent me a long letter. The letter described his life in Manchester and how he had changed as a person. It made me unsure of what to expect when he would return. Now, in the three weeks since his return, we have seen each other only once. I can't believe it, he is such a different person from the Peter who had left a year ago. Next month my friends are organizing a party for my twenty-first birthday and they want Peter and his friends to come along. My problem is trying to decide whether or not to invite Peter. I'm scared it could be a total disaster if I do. What do you suggest?

Heartbroken

Dear Heartbroken,

You poor girl you seem very upset. Peter sounds attractive with his independent spirit and curiosity about the world. But now that we live in a global village it is easy to understand his desire to study abroad. Everyone, 35 *however, has to expect that Peter would change. And although it might be sad, the people waiting his return have to see this change as natural. I mean if he didn't change, then there wouldn't have been any reason for him to go away, right? Perhaps the best clue to how he really feels can be found in the letter he wrote. I suggest you read it again and ask him to explain what* 40 *he meant if you feel uncertain about what he was trying to tell you. About the twenty-first party, I think you should invite him but don't count on him too much. If he decides not to attend, then you shouldn't take it personally. After all, he is the one who has changed. There's no doubt the next few months will be difficult, but keep in mind you are young and you have* 45 *plenty of other experiences to enjoy. Most of all, remember that no matter what, life must go on.*

Jane Sanders

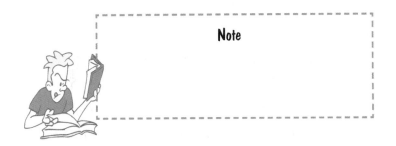

Note

Multiple Choice

—— 1. Jane Sanders is someone to write to ————.

    (A) for advice in personal matters

    (B) whenever you feel like it

    (C) whenever there is the prospect of disaster

    (D) when you are full of complaints about government's policies

—— 2. One of the reasons why the girl loved Peter is ————.

    (A) that Peter promised to take her to the United Kingdom with him

    (B) that she knew Peter would change into a better man after he finished the study in the United Kingdom

    (C) because of his enthusiasm and interest towards everything in the world

    (D) because Jane Sanders believed that Peter would make a good match for the girl

—— 3. When Peter first told his girlfriend he would study in the United Kingdom, she ————.

    (A) didn't let him go

    (B) understood his reasons for leaving

    (C) was heartbroken

    (D) knew he would change after he came back

—— 4. When Peter first arrived in the United Kingdom, ————.

    (A) not everything happened as they planned

    (B) he wrote his girlfriend a letter every day

    (C) he already had decided to break up with his girlfriend

    (D) he and his girlfriend communicated regularly

—— 5. Peter changed ————.

    (A) after he returned from the United Kingdom

    (B) while he was in the United Kingdom

    (C) while he was away, then changed again when he returned

    (D) into a man without enthusiasm and interest towards everything

—— 6. Peter's girlfriend is unsure if she ———————.

    (A) should invite him to her party because he studied in Manchester

    (B) should invite him to her party

    (C) should have her twenty-first birthday party

    (D) should attend Peter's twenty-first birthday party

—— 7. Peter's girlfriend signs herself as "Heartbroken" because ———————.

    (A) she has heart disease

    (B) Peter has changed and their relationship isn't as close as before

    (C) it may make Jane Sanders take this letter more seriously

    (D) she and Peter broke up a few years ago

—— 8. Jane Sanders thinks it's understandable that ———————.

    (A) Peter is heartbroken

    (B) the party should proceed

    (C) Peter still loves his girlfriend

    (D) Peter has changed

—— 9. Jane Sanders says reading the letter ———————.

    (A) is the way to find out if Peter will go to the party or not

    (B) is the best way to make him explain the situation

    (C) and crying again can make the girl feel better

    (D) will provide the best clue to how Peter really feels

—— 10. The advice Jane Sanders gives ———————.

    (A) will probably mean Peter will be invited to the party

    (B) will not make a difference because it will probably be ignored

    (C) should be followed by all newspaper readers

    (D) will make the girl cancel the party

Try This!

The word in the center of each bracket is related to its surrounding words except one. Find the odd word out.

send

write   message

COMMUNICATE

share   exchange

reason

heartbroken

personal   worried

UPSET

sad   anxious

unhappy

wish

doubt   request

DESIRE

choose   hope

want

enthusiasm

self   free

INDEPENDENT

unattached   alone

single

Key Words

clue *n.* 線索

count on 指望

curiosity *n.* 好奇心

describe *v.* 描述

desire *n.* 慾望

disaster *n.* 不幸

enthusiasm *n.* 熱忱

gradually *adv.* 漸漸地

heartbroken *adj.* 傷心的

occasionally *adv.* 有時

plenty *n.* 大量

prospect *n.* 展望

uncertain *adj.* 不確定的

upset *adj.* 煩亂的

珍‧姍德絲妳好

假如你有私人的問題，不知道要向誰求助，不妨寫信給報社的珍‧姍德絲，她是感情事務的專家。

珍‧姍德絲妳好：

我是二十歲的大學生，我四年前跟一個男生開始約會，他比我大一歲，中學的最後幾年，我們走得很近，我倆都覺得我們彼此相愛，我愛彼得的其中一個原因是因為他對世間一切事物都很有熱忱，因此他跟我說他計畫到英國讀一年書的時候，我也不覺得意外。當然我不希望他離開，不過我知道他對這個計畫很堅決，而且我們兩個都知道這一段經歷對他將來找工作很有幫助，他走的時候，我們說好要多寫電子郵件或是常常寫信，寫些重要的事情，我們也決定要偶爾打電話給對方。一開始的時候，我們的聯絡就跟原先計畫的一樣，不過慢慢地，什麼都變了，電子郵件幾乎都是我在寫，電話也都是我打的，後來就在他要回來之前，他寄了一封長信給我，信上說到他在曼徹斯特的生活，還有他變成了怎麼樣的一個人，讓我沒有把握他回來的時候會看到什麼樣子的他。而今，自從他回來之後三個禮拜，我們只見過一次面，真不敢相信，他跟一年前離開的彼得簡直就是判若兩人。下個月我朋友要開派對替我過二十一歲的生日，她們要彼得還有他的朋友一起來參加，我的難題就是要決定到底該不該邀請彼得，我很怕這麼一來，一切都會搞砸，妳有什麼建議嗎？

心碎的人

心碎的人妳好：

可憐的女孩，妳好像很煩，彼得聽起來很有魅力，個性獨立，對世事又富好奇心，不過既然我們住在地球村，不難理解他要到國外唸書的渴望，可是大家也要有心理準備，彼得可能會因此而有所改變，雖然有點難過，可是等他回來的人要以平常心看待這種改變，我是說，假設他一點都沒有變，那他何必出國去，對吧？要知道他到底在想什麼，最好的線索也許就是他寫的那封信，我建議妳把信再看一次，如果妳不確定他想告訴妳的是什麼，那就請他解釋他的用意何在。至於二十一歲的生日派對，我想妳應該邀請他，不過不要把他看得太重要，如果他決定不要參加，也不要認為他是針對妳，再怎麼說，變的人是他。接下來幾個月一定不好過，不過要記住，妳還年輕，還有許多美好的經驗等著妳去享受，最重要的，不管結局如何，人生還是要繼續下去。

珍‧姍德絲

大聲說：我愛你！

★Danish 丹麥語：Jeg elsker dig!

★Dutch 荷蘭語：Ik hou van je!

★English 英語：I love you!

★Filipino 菲律賓語：Iniibig kita!

★French 法語：Je t'aime!

★German 德語：Ich liebe dich!

★Greek 希臘語：S'ayapo!

★Hawaiian 夏威夷語：Aloha wau ia 'oe!

★Italian 義大利語：Ti amo!

★Japanese 日語：Kimi o ai shiteru!

★Portuguese 葡萄牙語：Eu te amo!

★Spanish 西班牙語：Te amo!

★Russian 俄語：Ya tyebya lyublyu!

Unit 12

The Channel Tunnel

你知道現在只要搭火車就能橫渡英吉利海峽了嗎？

The Channel Tunnel

The English Channel is the stretch of water that separates England and France. In the past, it was said that being separated was a good thing for these two proud and culturally diverse countries. In modern times, however, the Channel has been regarded by many people as simply a nuisance for European travel and trade. These people say it is inconvenient to ship and fly   5 people and goods for such a short distance. When engineers agreed a tunnel could be built, they presented their plans to the politicians.

In 1986 the politicians of both countries signed a treaty to allow the construction of the Channel Tunnel to begin. The plan was actually to build three tunnels. The location chosen for the tunnels was under the fifty   10 kilometers stretch of the Channel between Folkestone in England and Coquelles in France. Work began separately from both sides of the Channel. The three tunnels were built at a distance of thirty meters apart. The two outside tunnels were drilled to a diameter of 7.6 meters and were designed to carry passenger and freight trains. The narrow middle tunnel was designed as   15 a service tunnel. It was drilled to a diameter of 4.6 meters. The service tunnel was built mainly to be used in case of emergency and for those workers who maintained the two transport tunnels. Every 375 meters a cross link was built to connect the three tunnels.

Special drills were built to dig the tunnels. These enormous machines   20 were made to cut through the hard chalk rock that was found below the Channel seabed. The speed of drilling depended on the different types of chalk rock that the drills had to work against. When the rock was hard, the drilling slowed down. On average, however, the tunnels were built at the rate of two hundred meters a week. During construction, satellite data was used to   25 keep the tunnels correctly aligned and to ensure that both the French and English sides of the tunnel would meet in the middle.

The digging went according to the plan and all the three tunnels were completed in four years. Once they were dug, the tunnels were lined with concrete and fitted with railway tracks, ventilation systems and communication equipment. At the same time, two huge passenger and freight terminals were built at the ends of the tunnel. Both the English and French terminals were built to a size almost the same as an international airport. "Eurotunnel," the company in charge of all tunnel construction and transportation, built their head office in the French terminal. 35

In 1995, the tunnel was opened for public and commercial use. The first dry connection between England and France now makes it possible to travel from London to Paris by train in three hours. Every day, thousands of passengers make the journey and are impressed with how quiet and smooth it is to travel under the Channel on the electric lines. The success of the 40 Channel Tunnel will certainly benefit millions of people in the future and inspire further great engineering projects.

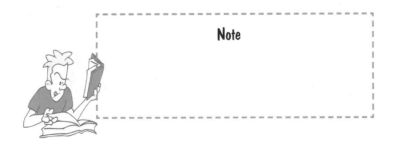

Note

True or False

——(1) France and England are separated by water known as the English Channel.

——(2) The Channel has been regarded as a nuisance for European travel and trade because it was inconvenient to ship and fly people and goods for such a short distance.

——(3) French and English politicians wanted the Channel Tunnel to be built but engineers didn't.

——(4) The French and English started building from separate sides of the Channel.

——(5) Three tunnels were built under the Channel, each separated by a distance of 375 meters.

——(6) Special drills were built to cut into the chalk rock found under the Channel.

——(7) Satellite equipment was used to ensure both sides of the tunnel would connect.

——(8) The English and French passenger and freight terminals were designed after international airports.

——(9) "Eurotunnel," the company in charge of all tunnel construction and transportation, built their head office in the British terminal.

——(10) The Channel Tunnel has been successful mainly because passengers are impressed by how quiet and smooth the ride is from Paris to London.

Try This!

Five of these headlines refer to "The Channel Tunnel." Each headline represents one paragraph. Write the paragraph number in the right order next to each correct headline and "wrong" next to the three paragraphs that don't belong to the subject.

Chalk Rock Creates
Headache for Drillers   (   )

International Airport Chosen Instead of Terminal   (   )

Not One...But THREE   (   )

Engineers Agree
Channel Tunnel
is "Possible"   (   )

**Eurotunnel Chooses
France Over England**   (   )

Passengers Agree on
Tunnel Dimensions   (   )

*Politicians Pleased With
Their "Tunnel Vision"*   (   )

Tunnel Dream Comes True   (   )

Key Words

align *v.* 排成直線	drill *v.* 鑽；*n.* 鑽孔機	satellite *n.* 衛星
apart *adv.* 分開地	freight *n.* 貨物	seabed *n.* 海床
chalk rock *n.* 白堊岩	inspire *v.* 鼓舞	stretch *n.* 廣大一片
channel *n.* 海峽	line *v.* 鋪襯	terminal *n.* 起站；終站
concrete *n.* 混凝土	narrow *adj.* 狹窄的	track *n.* 軌道
diameter *n.* 直徑	nuisance *n.* 妨害	treaty *n.* 條約
dig *v.* 挖掘	politician *n.* 政治家	tunnel *n.* 隧道
diverse *adj.* 不同的	present *v.* 呈現	ventilation *n.* 通風設備

英法海底隧道

英吉利海峽是分隔英、法兩國的一片海，在過去，大家都說分開來未嘗不是一件好事，因為這兩個國家十分高傲，文化的差異也很大；可是到了現代，很多人卻認為英吉利海峽對於歐洲的旅遊、貿易來說，簡直就是麻煩事，這些人表示，距離雖然短，但是要把人、貨物海運或是空運都很不方便，當工程師取得共識，認為建築海底隧道可行之後，他們就把計畫呈報給從政者。

1986年，兩國的從政者簽署一項條約，批准海底隧道的興建工程可以開始進行，這項計畫其實要建三條隧道，隧道的位置選在英國的福克斯頓和法國的康凱拉之間，在水面下橫越五十公里的海峽，工程由海峽的雙方分頭進行。這三條隧道建造時，兩兩相距三十公尺，兩側隧道挖掘的直徑是七點六公尺，設計給運送乘客和貨物的列車通過；中間的隧道比較窄，打算作為維修隧道之用，挖掘的直徑是四點六公尺，建造維修的隧道，主要是緊急事故發生時可以使用，也讓工人可以維修另外兩條運輸隧道；每隔三百七十五公尺，這三條隧道之間就建有相通的連結。

為了挖掘隧道，還建造了特殊的鑽孔機，這些大型機具是為了開鑿在英吉利海峽的海床所發現堅硬的白堊岩，而鑽孔的速度就要視白堊岩的種類而定。萬一岩石很堅硬的話，鑽孔的速度就會慢下來，不過平均起來，建造隧道的速度是每週兩百公尺，施工期間，衛星資料也派上用場，用以保持隧道精準地排列，確保英、法雙方建造的隧道到了中間能夠相連。

挖掘工作依計畫進行，三條隧道在四年內完工。隧道開挖之後，內部鋪上混凝土、鋪設鐵軌，也加裝了通風系統和通訊設備，在此同時，隧道兩端建了兩座大型的客貨兩用車站，英、法兩國的車站幾乎跟國際機場一樣大。負責隧道所有施工、運輸事務的「歐洲隧道公司」把他們的總公司設在法國的車站。

　　1995年隧道開放，供大眾和商業使用，是英、法雙方首次的陸路連結，現在三個小時內就可以從倫敦搭火車到巴黎，每天都有好幾千名乘客到此一遊，他們對於搭列車橫跨海峽下方竟然可以如此安靜平穩，都感到印象深刻，海底隧道的成功，今後絕對可以嘉惠無數的人，也為之後偉大的工程計畫帶來啟發。

隧道公司抱怨不公平

　　隧道經營公司對法國一家法庭說，非法移民試圖通過海底火車隧道進入英國的企圖嚴重影響了火車的正常運營，使公司每年蒙受巨額經濟損失。這家公司還對英國政府有關發現一個非法移民就對該公司罰款2,000英鎊的規定提出了抗議。公司的發言人說：「我們僅僅是一個私營公司，不是邊防檢查站。我們正在治安方面花費大筆的金錢，而英國政府卻不做貢獻，只是威脅對我們罰款。」

　　法國加來港口的工作人員說，由於海底隧道加強了保安措施，愈來愈多的非法移民正試圖採用更危險的方式，從海上到達英國。 在一起事件中， 英國海岸警衛人員在多佛爾港附近海面扣留了5名乘橡皮船從法國到英國的避難申請者。

　　這五名據信來自俄羅斯或其他東歐國家的男子被截獲時，出現體溫過低的症狀。海岸警衛人員說：「很幸運，他們還活著。」

Hong Kong

經濟昌榮、車水馬龍，這就是24小時繁忙的香港。

Hong Kong

Hong Kong is one of the most beautiful cities in the world. It is a city filled with high rise apartment blocks and skyscrapers perched on the water's edge. Behind the spectacular buildings, there are mountainous peaks on the islands that make up Hong Kong. Each day, millions of people catch ferries across the harbors and drive over enormous bridges as they commute to work. Hong Kong is also one of the busiest financial cities in the world because of the thousands of companies that use it as their Asian headquarters. The six million residents of Hong Kong are mostly Cantonese, but there are also thousands of foreigners who live and work in the city. Because of its British history, many people can speak English although most people speak Cantonese. The street signs in Hong Kong are written in both Chinese and English and it is just as easy to find western food as is to find Cantonese food.

Hong Kong has an interesting history. In the 1840's and 1860's, the British fought trade wars in Hong Kong harbor against the Chinese. After the fighting and many years of negotiation, Britain and China made an agreement in 1898. They decided Hong Kong would remain a British colony but only for ninety-nine years. During this period of British control, Hong Kong became a business center with low taxation rates and little government influence. This is the reason why the shopping in Hong Kong has always been so good and why so many large companies decided to move to Hong Kong. In fact, whatever people want can be found in Hong Kong and sometimes the city is called the biggest shopping mall in the world. But these days things in Hong Kong are far more expensive than they used to be, so it is important to shop around to find the best prices. In Hong Kong it is common to haggle, meaning customers can usually negotiate a discount price with shopkeepers.

In 1997, the period of British rule ended and Hong Kong became a part of China once again. In the years since the handover, Hong Kong has been ruled separately from China under a "one country, two systems" status. Today Hong Kong retains its capitalist economy and is still a vital place of business in East Asia. Hong Kong also maintains its reputation of being a modern and efficient city. An example is the Hong Kong Airport that opened in 1998 which is now the biggest airport in the world. When passengers walk around the airport terminal buildings, they get a feeling of how people might live in the future. The high speed train from the airport into the city comes with a video screen for each passenger. Then once in the city, passengers can connect with a complex underground train system. But not all of Hong Kong is high-tech and western influenced. Hong Kong also features traditional Chinese markets and busy neighborhoods that are exactly like those found around China. All of these facts and contrasts make Hong Kong a unique and intriguing place.

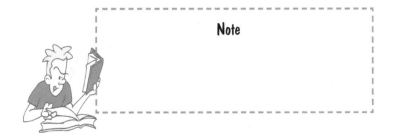

Note

Multiple Choice

—— 1. Hong Kong is one of the most beautiful cities in the world because _____.

(A) of its population

(B) of its natural and man-made scenery

(C) it is not a popular destination for tourists and businesspeople

(D) it isn't influenced by the West at all

—— 2. In Hong Kong, there are _____.

(A) only a lot of skyscrapers and apartment buildings

(B) few mountains but many tall buildings

(C) many mountains, skyscrapers and other tall buildings

(D) many beautiful mountains but only a few small and old buildings

—— 3. More people speak English _____.

(A) in Hong Kong than any other language

(B) in Hong Kong than in other parts of China because of the British influence

(C) in Hong Kong than in any other country

(D) in Hong Kong than in other parts of China because most of the residents are foreigners

—— 4. The British and Chinese fought wars _____.

(A) because they couldn't agree on the types of skyscrapers to be built

(B) just before the handover of British rule to Chinese rule

(C) because both wanted to control trade in the Hong Kong area

(D) in 1997 because of their desires to control Hong Kong

—— 5. Hong Kong remained a British colony _____.

(A) for ninety-nine years

(B) from 1899 to 1999

(C) for eighty-nine years

(D) from 1987 until 1997

—— 6. When the British first took control of Hong Kong, they ————.

    (A) made it difficult for foreigners to do business

    (B) built large, modern airports

    (C) forced everyone to speak English instead of Cantonese

    (D) tried to make Hong Kong a center of business

—— 7. Many companies set up their headquarters in Hong Kong because ————.

    (A) the shopping is so good

    (B) it's easy to haggle with shopkeepers

    (C) the Hong Kong Government influences international trade

    (D) of the low company taxation rates

—— 8. Hong Kong is not an independent country ————.

    (A) because the ninety-nine years of British rule ended

    (B) because political control was handed over from the British to the Chinese

    (C) at present because it is the headquarters of international trade

    (D) but it will be after ninety-nine years

—— 9. The new Hong Kong Airport is an example of ————.

    (A) the high-tech style of the city

    (B) how aircraft can land safely on mountains

    (C) the benefits of low taxation rates

    (D) traditional Chinese technology

—— 10. Hong Kong is often referred to as Canton（廣州）————.

    (A) because that is the heritage of its most people

    (B) because the shopping there is so great

    (C) by those who commute regularly to work in the city

    (D) because there are also many mountains in Canton

Try This!

Hong Kong is different from other countries in East Asia because it was directly ruled by an European country for most of its recent history. Put brackets around the following features of Hong Kong that can be directly related to the ninety-nine-year period of European rule.

low taxation rates make Hong Kong a financial center

English language understood by Hong Kong residents

government policy in Hong Kong after the 99 year agreement

political decision making from 1898–1997

natural landscape of the Hong Kong region

neighborhoods that retain their Chinese atmosphere

wars fought between the Chinese and the British in the 1840's and 1860's

the decision to build the new Hong Kong Airport

haggling for goods at market stalls

Chinese events such as Dragon Boat Festival

$$\boxed{\textbf{Key Words}}$$

Cantonese *n.* 廣東話

capitalist *adj.* 資本主義的

commute *v.* 通勤

discount *n.* 折扣

ferry *n.* 渡輪

haggle *v.* 討價還價

handover *n.* 移交

headquarters *n.* 總部

intriguing *adj.* 吸引人的

mall *n.* 購物中心

mountainous *adj.* 多山的

negotiate *v.* 溝通

peak *n.* 山頂

perch *v.* 坐落

resident *n.* 居民

retain *v.* 保持

skyscraper *n.* 摩天大樓

spectacular *adj.* 壯觀的

status *n.* 狀態

taxation *n.* 課稅

vital *adj.* 重要的

香港

　　香港是世界上最美麗的都市之一，公寓大樓鱗次櫛比，摩天大樓坐落在岸邊，華麗大廈的背後，香港其實是由許多山脊所組成的，每天都有幾百萬人通勤上班，有人是搭渡船橫越港口，也有人開車通過大橋。香港也是世界上非常繁忙的商業城市之一，因為很多公司把香港當成亞洲總部。全香港六百萬居民中，多半是廣東人，不過在香港定居、工作的外國人也有數千人，雖然大多數人講廣東話，但由於有英國殖民的歷史，很多人也會講英語，香港街上的告示牌都是中英文並列，而且要找西式食物就跟廣式食物一樣容易。

　　香港的歷史耐人尋味，1840和1860年代，英國為了貿易，在香港的港灣和中國打仗，戰後經過多年的談判，中、英雙方於1898年達成協議，決定香港成為英國的殖民地，不過期限只有九十九年。英國統治期間，由於稅率低廉、政府干預不多，香港一躍而成商業中心，香港之所以是購物天堂，而且這麼多大公司決定遷到香港，就是這個原因。其實不管要什麼，都可以在香港找到，有時候還有人戲稱香港是全世界最大的購物中心，不過近年來，香港的東西比以前貴了不少，所以要貨比三家才能買到好價錢，在香港討價還價是家常便飯，也就是說顧客通常可以跟老闆要個折扣。

　　1997年，英國的統治時期結束，香港再度回歸成中國的一部分，自從移交之後的這幾年，香港受到中國個別的統治，在「一國兩制」之架構下，今天香港還保有資本主義經濟制度，依然是東亞的商業重鎮，香港還保有現代化、有效率之都的美譽，其中一個例子就是1998年啟用的香港機場，是現今全球第一大的航空站。乘客在航站大廳走動時，會覺得未來的生活如現眼前，從機場到市中心的高速火車上，每個乘客都有一個電視螢幕，一到市區，乘客還可以轉搭錯綜的地下鐵系統。不過

也不是全香港都是高科技或是受到西方影響，香港的特色也包括傳統的中國市場和
熱鬧的街坊，就和中國各處看到的一模一樣，這些現象和強烈的對比造就了香港這
個奇特的魅力之都。

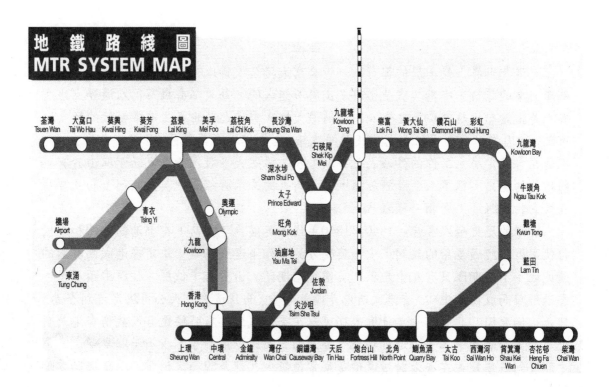

14 *Choosing a New Camera*

你還在看我嗎？
選一臺好相機，把帥帥的我拍下來吧！

Choosing a New Camera

Taking good photographs is a skill that takes many years to acquire. However, before you can even start learning photography, you need to have the right camera. If you are thinking about buying a new camera, then consider the following.

The most popular type of camera is the automatic camera. With an automatic camera, you only need to point the lens at your subject and press the button. This type of camera focuses automatically and flashes when there isn't sufficient light. Other common features include "Self-timer," which allows you to set up the camera so that it will take a photo by itself. "Red-Eye Reduction" takes away the red color normally seen on people's eyes when a flash is used. Automatic cameras are also popular because they are cheap and easy to carry.

The disadvantage of using automatic cameras is that you don't get much choice in the type of photograph you can take. For example, if you are far away from an object, you won't be able to photograph in detail. To do this, you need a zoom lens. Another disadvantage of an automatic camera is the lack of control you have over focusing. Perhaps you want to have the background in sharper focus than the foreground. With an automatic camera this is impossible. There is also the problem of taking photos at night. To do this successfully, you need to have a slow shutter speed on your camera. But on automatic cameras you can not adjust the shutter speed.

If you want more control over your photographs, you should use a "Single-Lens Reflex" (SLR) camera. In fact, serious photographers only use SLR cameras because they can adjust the lens, the focus and the shutter speed when they take photos. The different lenses you can use include wide-angle lenses, telephoto lenses and zoom lenses. If you own a SLR camera, you can buy many lenses and use each one depending on the type of photo you want to take. The SLR cameras are larger, heavier and more expensive than the

5

10

15

20

25

automatic cameras and they come with more equipment.

Automatic cameras and SLR cameras are common but they aren't the 30 only types of camera available. Disposable cameras are cheap cameras that only take one roll of film. These are good to use when you photograph in a place where your good camera may get damaged from water, sand or heat. Another type is the instant camera. Instant cameras are good and fun to use at parties because the film develops inside the camera. Just five minutes after 35 the photo has been taken, you and your friends can be looking at the picture. Hand held video cameras are also getting cheaper and easier to use. If you are going traveling, perhaps a small video camera is better than a normal camera for taking photographs.

The best way for you to choose the right camera is to consider what 40 types of photographs you want to take. And of course, you can always have more than one camera if you want to take different types of photographs.

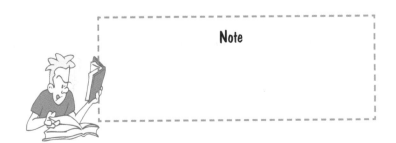

Note

True or False

—(1) Taking good photographs is very easy when you have the right camera.

—(2) Automatic cameras are popular because they are better than SLR cameras.

—(3) When using a flash to photograph a person, you should use the red-eye reduction and not the self-timer.

—(4) An automatic camera is good for taking pictures at night because you can adjust the shutter speed.

—(5) Good photographers don't use automatic cameras because they prefer having choices when they take photographs.

—(6) SLR cameras come with more equipment than automatic cameras but apart from that, there are no differences.

—(7) If you own a SLR camera, you can buy many lenses and use each one depending on the type of photo you want to take.

—(8) People should use disposable cameras because normal cameras break easily.

—(9) Instant cameras and video cameras should only be used for parties and traveling.

—(10) The type of camera you choose should depend on what type of photographs you want to take.

Try This!

Fill in the gaps with words from the box to make complete sentences.

| photographs | flash | lens | red-eye reduction | camera |
| self-timer | zoom | adjust | shutter | automatic |

1) An ——————— camera makes it easy for the photographer to keep the subject in focus.

2) It is essential to have a good ——————— with the right equipment to take quality photographs.

3) It is often necessary to use a ——————— for night photography.

4) Photographers who want to choose which ——————— to use should have a SLR camera.

5) ——————— ensures photographs of people will not be ruined by strange colors.

6) Night photography with a SLR camera may require adjustments to the ——————— speed.

7) If the photographer wants to be in his or her own photograph, the ——————— should be used.

8) To take a clear photograph of a faraway object, a ——————— lens may be beneficial.

9) The type of ——————— that you want to take will determine the type of camera you choose to buy.

10) Because professional photographers need to ——————— their equipment often, they will mostly use SLR cameras.

Key Words

acquire *v.* 學得
adjust *v.* 調整
angle *n.* 角度
disposable *adj.* 可丟棄的
flash *v., n.* 閃光
focus *v.* 對焦；*n.* 焦距
foreground *n.* 前景

instant *adj.* 立即的
lack *v.* 缺乏
lens *n.* 鏡頭
photography *n.* 攝影
press *v.* 按
reduction *n.* 修正
reflex *n.* 反射

self-timer *n.* 自拍裝置
sharp *adj.* 清晰的
shutter *n.* 快門
sufficient *adj.* 足夠的
telephoto *adj.* 長鏡頭的
zoom *n.* 自由焦距

挑選新相機

照片拍得好也是一種技巧，要花好幾年的時間才學得來，不過在你學習攝影之前，你必須先有一臺適合的照相機，假如你考慮買臺新相機，請你考慮以下幾點。

最受大眾青睞的機種是自動相機，有了自動相機，只要把鏡頭對準你要的目標，再按下快門就可以了，這類的相機會自動對焦，光線不足也會自動閃光；另一項常見的特點就是「自拍裝置」，只要將相機加以設定，它就會自動拍照；而通常使用閃光燈後，會發現人的眼中出現紅點，有了「防紅眼裝置」，問題就可迎刃而解。自動相機會這麼普遍，還包括價位不高與攜帶方便等原因。

自動相機的缺點就是你能拍的相片類型並不多，舉個例子來說，如果你距離目標很遠，就沒辦法把細部照清楚，要達到這種效果就需要伸縮鏡頭；自動相機的另一個缺點就是你沒有辦法調整焦距，也許你希望把焦點放在背景而不是前景，這用自動相機是辦不到的；夜間攝影也有問題，要在夜間拍攝成功，你的相機必須能放慢快門的速度，可是自動相機不能調整快門的速度。

假如你想將照片掌握得更好，你應該用「單眼相機」，其實要求很高的攝影師都只用單眼相機，因為照相的時候可以調整鏡頭、焦距和快門的速度。各種可以使用的鏡頭包括廣角鏡頭、長鏡頭、伸縮鏡頭等。如果有一臺單眼相機，你可以買各種鏡頭，使用的時機就看你想要拍哪一種照片。和自動相機比起來，單眼相機比較大、比較重，價格較高，而且配備也較多。

自動相機和單眼相機都很普及，不過也不是只有這兩種相機，即可拍相機很便宜，但是只能照一卷底片，如果不希望你的高級相機不小心浸水、跑進沙子、或因高溫而產生毀損，這時候即可拍相機最好用了；另一種就是拍立得相機，這類相機在聚會的場合最能增加樂趣，因為底片在相機裡頭馬上就能沖洗出來，照片照好以後只要五分鐘，你和你朋友就可以看照片了；至於手提錄影機，不但愈賣愈便宜，也愈來愈容易上手；你如果要去旅行，那麼小型的錄影機會比一般的相機要來得適合。

　　選相機最好的做法，就是要考慮到你想拍哪一種照片，假如你想要拍出各種不同類型的照片，當然你也可以多買幾臺相機。

數位相機

　　數位相機與傳統相機的原理幾乎沒什麼不同，同樣是利用光學鏡頭，將物體反射的光聚焦在相機的內部，唯一的差別在於這兩種相機所使用的成像材料不同。傳統相機是利用膠片，使光在感光劑上感光，發生化學變化。數位相機是不用裝底片的，而是使用CCD (Charge Coupled Device)的半導體感光材料。CCD的功能是透過鏡頭，把光信號轉變成強弱不同的電荷訊號，然後利用這些電荷訊號轉換成數位資料，拍攝的畫像可以經過信號傳送給電腦，記錄在記憶體上，儲存成電腦可以讀取的檔案。如果帶有TV輸出介面，還可以在電視螢幕上直接顯示出畫像。數位相機的品質決定於它的畫素。受光畫素愈多，圖像的清晰度愈高。數位相機技術發展日新月異，機種不斷推陳出新。不久的將來，將會取代傳統的膠片式照相機。

15 *Beach Excursion*

你想去什麼樣的海灘渡假呢 ？

Beach Excursion

Everyone had been looking forward to our class excursion to the coast. Our group consisted of nine people, eight students and our biology teacher, Mr. Harris. None of us knew what Mr. Harris had planned. All he said was that we could expect plenty of fun, plenty of work and we would learn something as well. After a five hour train ride from London to the west coast of England, we arrived at the small beachside town where we had booked to stay.

On the first morning, we woke up early and were happy to see the blue sky. It looked like a perfect day for the beach. Mr. Harris rented umbrellas so none of us would get sunburnt. In the morning we swam, played badminton and drank plenty of water to stay hydrated. Mr. Harris was very relaxed and we were pleased to realize he was a normal person as well as our high school science teacher. In the afternoon, Mr. Harris asked us if there was anything we didn't like about the beach. One of the boys, George, was the first to answer.

"The only thing I don't like is all the garbage scattered around the place," said George, and the rest of us agreed. The white sand, the blue ocean and green dunes was a nice environment and it seemed odd that people would leave garbage behind. Mr. Harris then began telling us about the ocean and its surrounding environment. He said most marine life lived very close to the water's edge and further out to sea was like an underwater desert where not much life could be found. That's why it was crucial to keep the coastal area clean and free of pollution.

"As you can see the beach is littered with aluminum cans, glass bottles, plastic bottles, plastic bags, batteries, cigarette butts and other garbage," said Mr. Harris. "All of that affects the birds, the fish, the sea plants and the rest of the ecosystem around the coast."

We had learnt in science class that ecosystems could only function if all parts of the food chain worked together. For example, if the sea plants died, there would be no food for the little fish; and if there were no little fish, the big fish would starve. 30

"What we need to do is clean up the beach," said Mr. Harris, "Any volunteers?" Now we understood the main reason for being here. We were all enthusiastic about working for the beach environment. All of us volunteered.

The next day at breakfast, we discussed our plan. We split up into four groups of two and each group worked on a separate part of the beach. Collecting the garbage was easy and Mr. Harris said we could go swimming whenever we felt hot. By the end of the day, our task was complete. We had filled ten large garbage bags between us. Unfortunately, we had to return to London the next afternoon. But while our group was leaving our hotel, an old man came over to us and said, "Throughout the year, people from all over England have been coming to this beach and often they leave their garbage behind. Thank you for cleaning up and disposing of their mess." 35 40

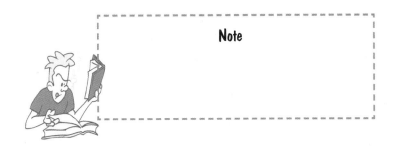

Note

Multiple Choice

—— 1. The group on the excursion consisted of ————.

    (A) eight biology teachers and their student

    (B) nine people and a dog

    (C) eight students and their biology teacher

    (D) nine students and a bus driver

—— 2. Mr. Harris was ————.

    (A) the leader of the class excursion to the coast

    (B) an expert on many things including garbage disposal

    (C) secretive about the excursion to the north coast of England

    (D) good at swimming and taught students how to swim

—— 3. The students spent their time ————.

    (A) working because the weather was nice

    (B) answering questions in biology class

    (C) collecting garbage and playing on the beach

    (D) enjoying the beauty of the beach because it was very clean

—— 4. The students were pleased to realize that ————.

    (A) Mr. Harris rented umbrellas for them

    (B) Mr. Harris was actually a normal person

    (C) Mr. Harris allowed them to swim in the ocean

    (D) Mr. Harris recovered the ecosystem

—— 5. George noticed that the beach was ————.

    (A) polluted with garbage

    (B) an odd place to have an excursion

    (C) a nice place to work with the other students

    (D) a good place to observe the ecosystem

—— 6. Mr. Harris told the students that —————.

    (A) most of the marine life lived far away from the coast

    (B) most of the marine life lived close to the coast

    (C) the ocean was an underwater desert

    (D) most of the marine life could be found in the underwater desert

—— 7. Garbage looks ugly —————.

    (A) and it also affects the ecosystem

    (B) because it affects the ecosystem

    (C) but does not have any other effects

    (D) only on the beaches

—— 8. Healthy ecosystems require —————.

    (A) an understanding of all parts of the food chain

    (B) people to keep them under control

    (C) all parts of the food chain to be living normally

    (D) people to produce more sea plants for little fish

—— 9. The students didn't mind collecting garbage because —————.

    (A) they wanted to stay together as a group

    (B) they would get some candies as reward

    (C) Mr. Harris was a very good science teacher

    (D) they thought they were working for a good cause

—— 10. The class excursion was a success —————.

    (A) but the local people took the cleanup for granted

    (B) because the ecosystem recovered immediately

    (C) but the main tasks remained incomplete

    (D) and the local people appreciated the cleanup

Try This!

Find words in the text which have a similar meaning to the words in the two lists.

From lines 1–23

short journey   _____

suppose   _____

hired   _____

not worried   _____

regular   _____

spread out   _____

ocean   _____

very important   _____

From lines 24–43

trash   _____

micro-environment   _____

die of hunger   _____

interested   _____

offer help   _____

gather   _____

job   _____

throwing away   _____

Key Words

aluminum *n.* 鋁	edge *n.* 邊緣	odd *adj.* 古怪的
badminton *n.* 羽毛球	enthusiastic *adj.* 熱心的	rent *v.* 租
book *v.* 預定	excursion *n.* 短程旅行	scatter *v.* 散播
butt *n.* 菸蒂	function *v.* 起作用	split *v.* 分開
crucial *adj.* 重要的	hydrate *v.* 與水化合	starve *v.* 飢餓
dispose *v.* 處理	litter *v.* 使散亂	sunburn *v.* 日曬
dune *n.* 沙丘	marine *adj.* 海洋的	task *n.* 差事
ecosystem *n.* 生態系統	mess *n.* 髒亂	volunteer *n.* 自願者

海濱之旅

　　大家都很期待要到海邊班遊，我們這群是由九個人組成，八個學生加上我們的生物學老師哈利斯先生，沒有人知道哈利斯先生有什麼安排，他只說絕對樂趣無窮，而且有很多工作要做，還能學到一些東西。從倫敦搭了五個小時的火車前往英國的西海岸之後，終於來到一個海濱小鎮，我們已經在那裡訂房過夜。

　　隔天早晨我們起得很早，看見藍藍的天，心中暢快無比，那天看起來正是適合到海邊玩的日子，哈利斯先生租了陽傘，這樣才不會有人曬傷。我們早上就游游泳、打打羽毛球，還喝了很多水以防脫水，看到哈利斯先生非常悠哉，我們都很高興知道他和一般人沒什麼兩樣，雖然他也是我們的高中自然科學老師。下午的時候，哈利斯先生問我們，在這海邊有沒有什麼地方是我們看不順眼的，我們當中的喬治首先回答。

　　喬治說：「只有一件事情我不喜歡，就是這個地方到處都是垃圾。」我們其他人也很認同，因為白沙藍海配上綠色的沙丘，是個宜人的環境，但是竟然會有人把垃圾留下來，真的是很奇怪。哈利斯先生開始跟我們聊起這片海洋以及周遭的環境，他說大部分的海洋生物都在近海生活，再往外海，就好比水中沙漠一樣，並沒有很多的生命，而保持沿海地區乾淨不受污染之所以非常重要，就是這個原因。

　　哈利斯先生還說：「你們也看到了，沙灘上到處是丟棄的鋁罐、玻璃瓶、塑膠瓶、塑膠袋、電池、菸蒂，還有其他的垃圾，這些東西會影響鳥類、魚類、海洋植物、還有沿岸其他的生態系統。」

　　我們上自然科學的時候曾經學過，只有在食物鏈的每一個環節都分工合作時，生態系統才能正常運作，舉個例子，如果海洋植物死掉了，小魚就沒有食物，而如果小魚沒有了，大魚也會跟著餓死。

哈利斯先生說：「我們要做的就是把海灘清乾淨，有人自願嗎？」現在我們終於了解來這裡最重要的原因了。能對海邊的環境盡一份心力，我們都很熱心，每個人都自願幫忙。

第二天吃早餐的時候，我們就討論計畫，我們分成四組，一組兩人，每一組負責各自清理一部分的海灘。撿拾垃圾很輕鬆，哈利斯先生說只要我們覺得熱就可以去游泳，一天下來，任務圓滿達成，在大家共同努力之下，我們裝滿了十大袋的垃圾，只可惜我們第二天下午就得回倫敦了。不過就在我們一行人要離開旅館的時候，有個老人過來跟我們說：「一年到頭，全英國的人都會來這個海灘，往往只會留下垃圾，不過謝謝你們幫忙清理，把他們留下來的爛攤子解決掉。」

Unit
16 *Good English*

原來學英文有這麼多方法啊！

Good English

English is used everywhere for travel, entertainment, information and business. This means people who want to be successful in international settings must be able to comprehend and communicate a very good level of English. Here are a few ideas for how to take your English skills to the next level.   5

Most people know the fundamental words in English. The challenge, therefore, is to improve your English to a standard that can be used in all situations. To get to this level, you need to be determined and serious about English. Of course you should understand that there will be difficulties along the way, but you must be optimistic about your ability to make it in the end.   10 Don't expect to be able to speak English fluently from the start. This is an unrealistic goal and will only lead to frustration. The best approach is to work at a consistent rate and have confidence that over some time your English will steadily improve. Keep in mind that in two years your English will be much better than it is now. In five years it will probably be excellent.   15

You can learn English pronunciation from the words in songs or from the dialogs in movies. English words are also commonly read in magazines and newspapers and heard on television. The Internet has millions of websites in English, and with email you don't have to try hard to find fellow correspondents who are native English speakers. Reading English books and   20 magazines instead of what you normally read will expose you to thousands of words and vastly improve your English vocabulary and spelling. Whenever you read or hear a new word, no matter how obscure it sounds, you should jot it down and learn it. When you begin to look for English in this way, you will find new words everywhere.   25

As with any other challenge you undertake, you should set yourself a goal. Probably the best goal for learning English is a reward like traveling in an English-speaking country. For example, you may decide to learn English intensively for six months and at the end of that time, take a trip to Scotland. When you have something like this to look forward to, you will certainly make great improvements. When you travel to a country like Scotland, you will have many chances to practice your English as it is likely that not many Scottish people will have the ability or confidence to speak your language. In some circumstances, you may actually be forced to speak English to save money and survive. After returning from such a trip, you will be pleasantly surprised at how much progress you have made.

30

35

Once you can understand and speak English, you have a valuable skill that you can use for the rest of your life. At work, it will open doors for you that otherwise might have remained closed. It will help you appreciate the expanding world of English language entertainment and information. It will also let you feel confident about studying, traveling and working in most countries in the world. One thing is certain, English is going to stay the world language for some time. Make sure you are willing and able to communicate.

40

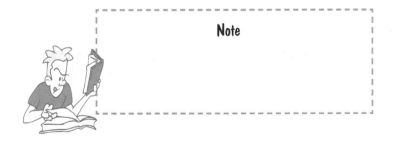

Note

Multiple Choice

—— 1. English ————.

    (A) is so far the world language, but it won't be so next year

    (B) is always taught by native English speakers

    (C) is used only in English-speaking countries

    (D) is used everywhere for travel, entertainment, information and business

—— 2. People who want to be successful in international settings ————.

    (A) should be comfortable communicating in a good standard English

    (B) should go to every English-speaking country

    (C) can choose which language will be essential for world business

    (D) should be able to master English within a year

—— 3. It is easy to know the fundamentals of English ————.

    (A) because most people enjoy communicating with easy words

    (B) but unacceptable to know any more than that

    (C) by reading English newspapers without the help of dictionary

    (D) if you have studied the language for a few years

—— 4. If you think you will be able to speak fluent English from the start, ————.

    (A) you are being unrealistic and will probably become frustrated

    (B) you will succeed because English is an easy language

    (C) you must be a very generous person

    (D) you can emigrate to any country without any problem

—— 5. Thinking about your future language ability ————.

    (A) helps you believe you will improve

    (B) will make you struggle in class

    (C) is not recommended for people who can speak basic English

    (D) will make you feel discouraged

—— 6. You can learn English pronunciation ——————.

(A) by reading English stories

(B) with your classmates by chatting with each other in English

(C) by looking up words in a dictionary

(D) from the words in songs or from the dialogs in movies

—— 7. English magazines are good for learning English ——————.

(A) because they force you to learn the new vocabulary that you find

(B) because they contain many words that are commonly used

(C) but only if they are read every day

(D) because all the articles have translations

—— 8. Having a goal to travel to an English-speaking country ——————.

(A) is not a good idea for people who are not native English speakers

(B) will provide the motivation to find a job there as well

(C) will provide the motivation to keep you working hard with your English

(D) is unpractical because it will cost you a lot of money

—— 9. English is valuable because ——————.

(A) it's a skill that people seldom use

(B) it opens many opportunities that otherwise may have remained closed

(C) only people in English-speaking countries understand the language

(D) everyone in the world can speak it

—— 10. If you can already communicate in good English, ——————.

(A) there is certainly no need to continue trying to improve

(B) you should probably keep trying to learn new words when you see them

(C) you will be able to understand every English word in the dictionary

(D) it's alright to forget your mother language

Try This!

English is written and spoken in different styles depending on its context. Read the following extracts and write which context they come from. The contexts are either: newspaper, letter, travel, business, email, novel or job interview.

1) On Wednesday I'll be at the Cyberhouse Internet café at two o'clock in the afternoon, so perhaps we should meet there. Send me a message to confirm if you can make it. ———————

2) "I think we are getting close to concluding the deal. Once the contract is accepted and signed by both companies, we will be able to process the account." ———————

3) "In this position, you will be expected to build websites and write marketing proposals for our customers. Do you think you have enough experience to meet these challenges?" ———————

4) Jerome followed his younger friend down the crowded street, his thoughts were playing over the conversation they were about to have. He wondered if this was the right time to tell him about what he had seen in the apartment the day before. ———————

5) I apologize for not having written to you for so long. As usual, I have been up to my neck in work. And now that I am soon to be married, so I barely have time for anything. ———————

6) Ian Rand, the police chief in charge of the investigation, yesterday said the chances of catching those responsible for the diamond theft had greatly improved. "We have new evidence that will allow us to positively identify the suspects," he told a busy news conference yesterday. ———————

Key Words

approach *n.* 方法
comprehend *v.* 了解
consistent *adj.* 經常不變的
correspondent *n.* 通信者
determined *adj.* 堅決的
expand *v.* 擴大
expose *v.* 使暴露
fellow *n.* 同伴

fluently *adv.* 流利地
frustration *n.* 挫折
fundamental *adj.* 基本的
intensively *adv.* 密集地
jot *v.* 匆匆記下
level *n.* 程度
obscure *adj.* 不清楚的
optimistic *adj.* 樂觀的

pronunciation *n.* 發音
Scotland 蘇格蘭
setting *n.* 環境
standard *n.* 標準
steadily *adv.* 不斷地
survive *v.* 生存
undertake *v.* 承擔
vastly *adv.* 大大地

學好英文

　　不管到哪裡去旅遊、玩樂、交換資訊或是經商，英文都派得上用場，也就是說，想在國際社會出人頭地，英文的理解、溝通能力一定要達到相當高的水平，以下幾個方法，可以將你的英文能力提升到另一個境界。

　　英文中的基本單字，大多數的人都會，所以最大的困難，是把英文加強到一定的標準，在什麼場合都能運用自如。要達到這種境界，就得下定決心，認真學英文，但你應該可以想見，一路上必定困難重重，不過也要對自己的能力抱持樂觀的態度，相信自己最後一定能做到。不必要求自己一開始就能用英文侃侃而談，這樣的目標不切實際，只會徒增挫折，最好的方法是循序漸進，相信自己的英文能夠與時並進，只要記住，兩年內，你的英文一定比現在好很多；五年內，就有可能變得非常厲害。

　　英文歌詞或是電影對話中，都可以學到英文發音，報章雜誌上也常常看到英文字，電視上也常聽到英文，網路上更有無數的英文網站，只要寫一寫電子郵件，不難找到以英文為母語的同好做朋友。不要只是閱讀平常習慣的語文，改讀英文書籍、雜誌，沉浸在英文字海當中，可以大大擴充英文字彙，並且提升拼字能力，只要看到或聽到生字，任憑它聽起來再奇怪，都要趕緊寫下來並加以學習，一旦用這種方法學習英文之後，你會發現無處不是新字。

　　正如同面對其他挑戰一樣，學英文也要給自己設定目標，也許學英文最棒的目標就是犒賞自己到英語系的國家玩一玩，好比說你已經下定決心，要用六個月的時間密集地學英文，學到最後，就可以到蘇格蘭去旅行，有了這一類的誘因，你的英文一定會進步神速。到了蘇格蘭這樣的國家，有很多練習英文的好機會，因為可能沒有多少蘇格蘭人會說，或是敢說你的語言，有些情況下，你可能為了省錢或是為了活命，還不得不說英文，這樣一趟旅行回來，看到自己的英文進步這麼多，肯定又驚又喜。

　　一旦你學會英文，可以琅琅上口以後，英文就成了一生受用無窮的技能，就業時，可以開啟很多扇大門，不然這些門可能是緊緊關著的；而英語的娛樂、資訊市場也在成長，學會英文能讓你沉浸其中，另外，也讓你有信心到世界上大多數國家去唸書、旅遊或是工作。有一件事情是肯定的，英文是世界通用的語言，短期之內不會改變，所以務必敞開心胸，學好這項溝通的利器。

挑戰英語大舌頭

1. The sixth Chief's sixth sheep was sick.

2. She sells seashells at the seashore.
   Seashells she sell sat the seashore.
   At the seashore she sells seashells.

3. Peter Piper picked a peck of pickled peppers.
   If Peter Piper picked a peck of pickled peppers,
   where is the peck of pickled peppers Peter
   Piper picked?

Unit 17

Australian Aboriginal People

駐足聆聽曠野的聲音⋯
他們是一群與自然和諧共存的生命體。

Australian Aboriginal People

Experts are uncertain when the Aboriginal people first arrived in Australia. Some estimate they arrived in Australia by boats from Indonesia 120,000 years ago. Others say they arrived 40,000 years ago. What experts do agree on is the fact that Aboriginal Australians remained isolated on the Australian continent for a very long time. Over that period they settled all over the land, from North to South and from East to West. Some lived around the forests and rivers of the southwest of Australia. Others lived five thousand kilometers away, around the tropical regions of the East Coast. Some groups lived in the mountainous areas and others lived in the hot dry deserts of central Australia. Because of this isolation, the various tribes formed their own customs and languages. It is estimated that the Aboriginal people spoke three hundred different languages.

The Aboriginal people developed a close connection to nature. Over thousands of years, they came to understand the behavior of animals and the cycles of plant life. The Aboriginal people did not get involved in farming, but instead lived by hunting and gathering. Often they used fire to burn down areas of forest and grassland. This encouraged new growth and attracted animals to their area. They also hunted animals such as kangaroos and emus with boomerangs and spears. In the northern wetlands, they made fish traps from bamboo and cord.

The Aboriginal people also developed a complex cultural life. Instead of writing their history, religion and law, the Aboriginal people told stories that were passed down from generation to generation. Sometimes they expressed their beliefs in songs and painted them on rock faces. Some of these stories explain how to find water in drought years and others describe the best places and times of the year to hunt.

Often the elders talk about the "Dreaming." This was a time when the earth, the plants, the animals and the people were created. The Dreaming

5

10

15

20

25

explains why the night sky is black and why the desert sand is red. It describes how snakes turned into rivers and how mountains grew from the earth. The "Dreaming" also explains how good and bad spirits live in the ground and in objects like trees and rocks. Many places in Australia such as Uluru (Ayers Rock) are sacred to the Aboriginal people. This is because of the connection these places have to stories in the Dreaming. ·30

In 1788, the English set up a small colony around Sydney harbor and claimed the continent as their own. Over the next fifty years, the English treated the Aboriginal people badly as they explored Australia. They took whatever land they wanted and expected the Aboriginal people to leave. The Aboriginal people could never fight against the English because they were peaceful people and lived in small separate groups. 40

These days, there are still problems between black and white Australians, usually involving land ownership. And because the Aboriginal people only make up two percent of the population, it is often they who lose the fight. Even though thousands of books have been written about the Aboriginal people, they still remain misunderstood by the majority of people in Australia. 45

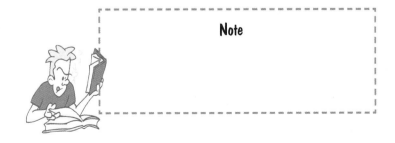

Note

Global Village English

True or False

——(1) Experts agree that the Aboriginal people have been isolated for a long time, but they don't agree about exactly how long they have been in Australia.

——(2) Aboriginal groups spread across Australia because they spoke different languages.

——(3) Hunting and gathering were the main ways the Aboriginal people fed themselves.

——(4) The Aboriginal people often used fire to burn down areas of forest and grassland to encourage new growth.

——(5) Stories passed down from generation to generation helped the Aboriginal people in their daily lives.

——(6) The Dreaming was discussed because it described where food could be found.

——(7) Some places in Australia are sacred because of their connection to stories in the Dreaming.

——(8) The English understood the Aboriginal people and their culture when they first arrived in Australia.

——(9) The Aboriginal people like to write books to tell others about their history.

——(10) Today black and white Australians get together very well.

Try This!

It is important to understand what is fact and what is theory when discussing topics such as Aboriginal culture. A fact is something that is true while a theory is just an idea that may or may not be true. Label the following sentences with "fact" or "theory."

———————— 1) The Aboriginal people have been in Australia for 120,000 years.

———————— 2) It is believed that the Aboriginal people lived in different parts of Australia.

———————— 3) Plants and animals played an important part in the lives of the Aboriginal people.

———————— 4) All Australian Aboriginal people knew how to hunt with spears and boomerangs.

———————— 5) Songs and paintings were often used by the Aboriginal people to express their beliefs.

———————— 6) Many places are sacred to Aboriginal Australians partly because of their connection to stories from the Dreaming.

———————— 7) The Aboriginal people had new problems after the English arrived in 1788.

———————— 8) The Aboriginal people could have forced the English to leave Australia if they were not peaceful people.

Key Words

bamboo *n.* 竹子	emu *n.* 鴯鶓	ownership *n.* 所有權
boomerang *n.* 迴力鏢	estimate *v.* 評估	sacred *adj.* 神聖的
continent *n.* 大陸	gather *v.* 採集	spear *n.* 長矛
cord *n.* 繩索	Indonesia 印度尼西亞	tribe *n.* 部落
custom *n.* 習俗	majority *n.* 大多數	tropical *adj.* 熱帶的
drought *n.* 乾旱	misunderstand *v.* 誤會	wetland *n.* 沼地

澳洲原住民

　　澳洲的原住民是什麼時候抵達澳洲的，專家也不確定，有的專家推估他們是十二萬年前，從印度尼西亞搭船到澳洲的，也有的專家說他們是四萬年前才到澳洲的，不過專家都同意，澳洲的原住民有很長一段時間，都孤立在澳洲大陸上。這段期間，他們在這片土地的四處定居，由北向南，由東向西，有些住在澳洲西南部的森林裡、河川旁，有些住在五千公里之外的東海岸熱帶地區，有些族群住在山區，也有些族群住在澳洲中部又熱又乾的沙漠，因為彼此孤立，各個部落衍生出自己的風俗、語言，據估計，原住民的語言多達三百種。

　　原住民和大自然發展出緊密的關係，幾千年來，他們慢慢了解動物的習性和植物的生長週期，這些原住民並不從事農業，而是仰賴狩獵和採集為生，通常都是放火焚燒森林、草地，這有助於植物的新生，進而引誘動物前來。他們也用迴力鏢和長矛獵殺袋鼠、鴯鶓等動物，在北部的沼澤區，他們還利用竹子和繩索做成捕魚的陷阱。

　　原住民還發展出一套繁複的文化生活，他們的歷史、宗教和法律不是用文字記載，而是以說故事的方式代代相傳，有時也會用歌謠述說他們的想法，或是把想法描繪在石面上，有些故事說明在連年乾旱時要怎樣找尋水源，有些則描述一年當中什麼時候要去哪裡打獵最好。

　　長老常常訴說一則「神話」，時間要回到大地、動植物與人類初創之時，這則「神話」解釋了為什麼夜晚的天空是黑的，為什麼沙漠的沙是紅的，還描述蛇變成河流、山岳從大地隆起的過程，也解釋善靈惡靈如何住在地底，以及住在樹木、石頭等物體裡。澳洲有許多地方，像是烏魯魯國家公園（艾耳斯巨岩所在地），都是原住民的聖地，因為這些地方和神話中的故事有所關連。

　　1788年，英國人在雪梨港附近建立一處小型的殖民地，並且聲明這片大陸歸他們所有，其後五十年，英國人在開發澳洲時，對待原住民的態度相當惡劣，除了對土地予取予求，還要求原住民遷離，但原住民無從對抗英國人，因為他們是愛好和平的一群人，而且只是散居各處的小部落。

　　近年來，澳洲的黑人和白人之間仍然有問題存在，通常牽涉到土地的所有權，而且因為原住民只占總人口的百分之二，在爭取土地的過程中，居下風的通常都是他們。即使與原住民的相關書籍已有數千本之多，但澳洲大多數人對於原住民仍然有所誤解。

文化滅絕的危機

　　在澳洲東南岸的大城市裏，澳洲原住民就好像隱形人，彷彿不曾存在這塊大陸似的，問問路人，他們總是朝內陸一指：「在叢林裡。」就算到了中澳這塊原住民的大本營，提到原住民，當地人總是蹙著眉頭，一股腦兒道出心中不滿：

　　「他們酗酒，老是醉眼迷離，在鎮上閒逛。」

　　「他們邋遢、愚蠢，穿得破破爛爛，但是口袋有錢。」

　　「政府給他們房子，他們把門窗拆來B.B.Q（烤肉），政府給他們的福利，比非原住民多了百分之三十。」

　　「水對他們而言不是拿來洗澡，他們又髒又臭，這裡做生意的人都怕『黑鬼』。」

　　「他們是絕種中的民族，無可救藥的文盲，沒有野心，沒有追求成功的欲望。兩百年了，他們還是沒辦法融入澳洲社會。」

　　面對大部分白人異樣的眼光，澳洲原住民也許並不在乎，他們最在乎的，卻是自己的文化、自己的種族會不會被同化，甚至滅絕。

　　在烏魯魯(Uluru)國家公園，也就是巨石艾爾斯岩所在地的遊客解說中心牆上，原住民的觀點這般陳述著：「政府的法律寫在紙上，我們的法律在我們的心裡、在我們的靈魂裡。我們不能把它寫成文字，因為那是祖先給我們的，我們要一直傳下去，用心、用靈魂……」。

Unit 18 The Titanic

Jack, don't go...   Jack...Jack...

The Titanic

The fate of the British Cruise Liner "Titanic" is one of the great disaster stories of the twentieth century. It's a story that has been retold over the years, written about in history books and made into Hollywood movies. It is so famous it has become a piece of modern folklore.

The Titanic was built to be the world's largest ship at a time when shipping was the main method of global transportation. When the ship was launched, it became the attention of world media. The designer of "Titanic," a man called Thomas Andrews, built the hull of the Titanic with sixteen watertight compartments. Because three of these compartments could be flooded without endangering the ship, many people believed the Titanic was unsinkable. The Titanic set out from its port in Southern England in 1912 and crossed the English Channel to France. Next it traveled to Ireland where it picked up the remaining passengers and made final preparations. The massive Titanic, two hundred and seventy meters long and nine decks high was finally ready to cross the Atlantic. On 11 April 1912, the Titanic set out on its maiden voyage to New York City.

The first days of the voyage were uneventful. But then on Sunday morning, April 14, the ship received a warning that icebergs lay ahead. Throughout the day, the Titanic kept its course until a call came to the Captain's Deck at 11:40 p.m. The call said "Icebergs right ahead!" The officer in charge ordered a turn and a complete stop but the order came too late. The Titanic crashed into a huge iceberg and was badly damaged. The designer Thomas Andrews was at the Captain's Deck when the damage reports came in. The reports were devastating, saying that five watertight compartments were flooded. At this point, Thomas Andrews knew the fate of the Titanic. He told Captain Smith that the Titanic would certainly sink.

The 2,227 passengers and crew were told of the imminent disaster. The lifeboats were loaded firstly with women and children but it was obvious that

there wasn't enough room for everyone. During the panic, the crew stayed at
their posts. The ship's orchestra continued to play and the maintenance crew   30
continued to work, making sure the lights of the ship stayed on until the very
last. Just after 2 a.m., the last lifeboat was launched and the remaining 1,500
passengers realized they were going to die. At 2:17 a.m., the Titanic broke
into two, the back half of the ship stood out of the water and then plummeted
to the bottom of the ocean. Not one of the lifeboats returned to rescue the   35
people who were drowning in the icy waters. At 4 a.m., a nearby ship arrived
after it heard the Titanic's distress signals on radio. All that remained of the
46,000 ton liner was a small collection of lifeboats and 705 freezing
survivors.

The next day, people throughout the world were shocked when they   40
heard the news. The ship that everyone thought was "unsinkable" had not
even completed its maiden voyage. Over 1,500 people had died and the
Titanic was a wreck on the ocean floor.

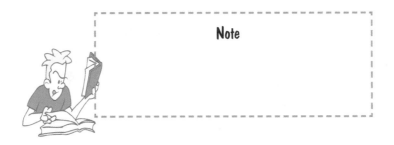

Note

Multiple Choice

—— 1. The story of the Titanic is well-known ————.

(A) because so many people were rescued from the ocean

(B) to all those who were on board

(C) because it has been retold in many forms

(D) because the main actor of the movie "Titanic" is very handsome

—— 2. The Titanic was thought to be unsinkable ————.

(A) but this theory turned out to be false

(B) especially when it was in the middle of the Atlantic Ocean

(C) because it was the world's longest ship

(D) because it was the world's most expensive ship

—— 3. When the Titanic was finally built, it sailed ————.

(A) to France, Ireland and then to New York

(B) out of its port and sank shortly afterwards

(C) directly to New York despite warnings given by Thomas Andrews

(D) from New York to France, and then to Ireland

—— 4. The Titanic didn't change course ————.

(A) when it was announced that icebergs were right ahead

(B) when it was first said that icebergs lay ahead

(C) when the captain realized that icebergs were immediately in front of the Titanic

(D) but icebergs did

—— 5. Thomas Andrews was ————.

(A) the captain of the ship

(B) so proud of his design that he wouldn't believe icebergs would damage his ship

(C) one of the musicians on the ship

(D) the designer of the ship

—— 6. The designer knew the fate of the ship —————.

    (A) once he knew the ship had hit an iceberg

    (B) as soon as the damage reports were brought to the captain

    (C) from the time the Titanic first left port

    (D) when it was announced that icebergs were right ahead

—— 7. As the ship began to sink, the passengers filled the lifeboats —————.

    (A) which were able to carry most of the people on board

    (B) and the orchestra played to make the maintenance crew work harder

    (C) but it soon became obvious that most passengers were going to die

    (D) and later came back to rescue the others who were drowning

—— 8. The rescue ship that arrived after the Titanic sunk —————.

    (A) was able to rescue most of the people who didn't get on the lifeboats

    (B) saw the final moments of the sinking ship

    (C) could only assist the people in the lifeboats

    (D) could have been there earlier if it had heard the Titanic's distress signals
       on radio

—— 9. People were shocked that the Titanic had sunk —————.

    (A) because the ship's construction had yet to be completed

    (B) because so many people had said it was unsinkable

    (C) but not really surprised because it was on its maiden voyage

    (D) because there were many rich people on the ship

—— 10. The Titanic —————.

    (A) contained sixteen watertight compartments

    (B) and all its passengers were all buried in the deep ocean

    (C) is still the world largest boat ever built

    (D) is actually a story made up by Hollywood

Try This!

Circle the odd words out (the first one has been done for you).

1) distress   danger   excite   upset

2) fate   help   future   destiny

3) panic   fear   alarm   reveal

4) huge   enormous   large   middle

5) rescue   save   die   assist

6) orchestra   instruments   violin   spear

7) launch   dinner   breakfast   snack

8) fall   plummet   drop   stop

9) signal   boat   ship   yacht

10) folklore   myth   newspaper   legend

Key Words

Atlantic *n.* 大西洋

captain *n.* 船長

compartment *n.* 船身隔間

course *n.* 航線

crew *n.* 工作人員

cruise *v.* 巡航

deck *n.* 甲板

distress *n.* 危難

endanger *v.* 危及

folklore *n.* 民間傳說

hull *n.* 船身

iceberg *n.* 冰山

imminent *adj.* 迫切的

launch *v.* 下水

lifeboat *n.* 救生艇

liner *n.* 遊輪

load *v.* 裝載

maiden *adj.* 處女的

maintenance *n.* 保養

massive *adj.* 宏偉的

orchestra *n.* 樂團

panic *n.* 驚惶

plummet *v.* 垂直落下

post *n.* 崗位

rescue *v.* 解救

sink *v.* 下沉

uneventful *adj.* 平靜無事的

unsinkable *adj.* 不沉的

watertight *adj.* 不進水的

wreck *n.* 殘骸

鐵達尼號

英國「鐵達尼號」遊輪的命運，是二十世紀一則非常悲慘的故事，這麼多年來，這個故事一再流傳，歷史書籍中也有提及，還拍成好萊塢的電影，可說是一則家喻戶曉的當代傳奇。

建造鐵達尼號的目的，就是要成為世界上最大的一艘船，當時水運正是全球運輸的主要方式，該船下水啟航時，成了全球媒體矚目的焦點。「鐵達尼號」的設計師是一個名叫湯馬士·安德烈斯的人，他以十六個防水的船艙打造鐵達尼號的船身，就算其中三個船艙淹水，也不會有什麼危險，因此許多人相信鐵達尼號是不會沉沒的。1912年，鐵達尼號從英國南部的港口出航，越過英吉利海峽而後抵達法國，接著又航向愛爾蘭搭載其餘的乘客，並做最後的準備工作。最後，巨大的鐵達尼號（長兩百七十公尺，高九層甲板）準備就緒，即將橫渡大西洋，在1912年四月十一日那天，鐵達尼號展開前往紐約市的處女航。

航行的頭幾天平靜無事，可是到了四月十四日星期天的早晨，船隻接獲警告，說之後的路上有冰山，那一整天，鐵達尼號維持原航線，直到晚上十一點四十分，有通報傳到船長室，通報中提到「冰山就在正前方」。負責的船員下令轉向，並全面停止前進，可惜這個命令下得太遲了，鐵達尼號撞上龐大的冰山，嚴重受損。損失報告傳回船長室時，設計師湯馬士·安德烈斯也在場，報告內容慘不忍睹，有五個防水艙淹水，這時，湯馬士·安德烈斯對鐵達尼號的命運已心裡有數，他告訴史密斯船長，鐵達尼號勢必沉沒。

　　兩千兩百二十七名乘客和船員聽到這項突如其來的噩耗後，就先讓婦女、小孩搭上救生艇，不過顯然救生艇的空間不夠，無法拯救每個人。人心惶惶之際，船員仍堅守崗位，船上的樂隊繼續演奏，維修人員也加緊搶修，務使船上的燈光能持續到最後一刻。凌晨兩點一過，最後一艘救生艇離開，剩下的一千五百名乘客，知道他們離大去之期不遠；凌晨兩點十七分，鐵達尼號一裂為二，船身後半部浮立水面，然後垂直下沉到海底，這些人在冰冷的海水中眼看就要溺斃了，卻沒有半艘救生艇回來營救。凌晨四點，一艘在附近的船隻，聽到鐵達尼號的無線電求救信號後前來，四萬六千噸的遊輪，最後只剩下為數不多的救生艇，和七百零五名快凍僵的生還者。

　　翌日聽到這個消息，舉世震驚，大家本以為「不會沉」的船，竟然連處女航都無法克竟全功，有一千五百多人喪命，而鐵達尼號也成了海底的一堆殘骸。

Environmental Damage

烏煙瘴氣……這就是我們住的地球嗎？

Environmental Damage

The earth is under enormous pressure. With a population of six billion people, the natural resources of the earth are being used up quickly. Lakes and rivers in all countries are being polluted and trees are being chopped down. Factories producing disposable goods for human consumption are pumping out harmful contamination into our skies. Every day, millions of people are causing extra pollution by driving their own cars instead of sharing rides with other people or taking public transportation. Of course it's impossible to prevent all pollution because people need to live their lives. However, it is essential that people are aware of how badly the earth is being damaged. Hopefully with greater understanding, people will put more effort into what they do to help the environment.

Global warming means that we are experiencing a gradual increase of the average temperatures on earth. The reason for higher temperatures is predominantly due to the burning of coal, oil and other fossil fuels for energy. Warmer temperatures mean the weather patterns we currently think of as normal could be dramatically altered in the future. If the temperatures continue to rise as they have done, then the polar ice caps in the Arctic and Antarctic regions will melt. The result would be a rise in the water levels, causing floods in coastal areas around the world. Global warming also means higher water temperatures in the oceans. The consequence of this is more frequent and more powerful storms and hurricanes.

Forests are another precious resource under threat. By producing enormous amounts of oxygen, trees and plants make it possible for people to breathe. Forests also maintain healthy soil and prevent floods by helping water absorb into the earth. But when a forest is destroyed, many species of plants, trees, insects and animals lose their habitats and may become extinct. Consider how valuable our forests are! It seems pointless to chop down millions of trees to produce disposable items such as newspapers.

In the twenty-first century, we are all faced with serious environmental problems. People must be more careful with how they consume and dispose of resources, and companies will have to follow much tighter regulations. Fortunately, many companies are discovering they can save money by following environmentally safe practices. Another good sign is that the recycling industry is becoming more profitable and money is being made by turning used products into new products.

Some countries are setting a good example in environmental protection. Germany, for example, is the world leader in environmental protection and awareness. When you enter a German supermarket, you will notice that most items come with little packaging. The cost of throwing away garbage in Germany is also very high, so people always try to reduce their waste and recycle as much as possible. Unfortunately, however, most people, companies and governments in other countries seem to have little respect for the environment. It is shocking to see them continue to pollute the earth in such a selfish and dangerous way.

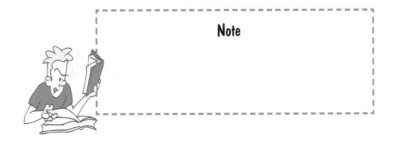

Note

True or False

——(1) The earth is under great pressure because so many people are using its resources.

——(2) Everybody needs to know about environmental damage because that will make them try harder to help the earth when they can.

——(3) Global warming may result in floods around coastal areas in the future.

——(4) Warmer ocean temperatures will kill all fish and result in starvation.

——(5) People who live near forests that are chopped down are no longer able to breathe.

——(6) Besides producing oxygen, forests also prevent floods and provide animals with proper habitats.

——(7) The way we live will be different in the future; and therefore, the way we currently damage the environment must not continue.

——(8) It is impossible to make money from practicing environmentally friendly methods.

——(9) Germany, for example, is the world leader in environmental destruction.

——(10) Many people, companies and governments are still polluting the earth in a dangerous way.

Try This!

Place the following words or phrases into three categories: cause, effect and solution.

factory contamination   use clean energy   forests chopped down

use public transportation   global warming   burning fossil fuels

car pollution   reduce consumption   poor soil

powerful storms   floods   recycle waste

Cause	Effect	Solution

Key Words

absorb *v.* 吸收	dramatically *adv.* 巨大地	pattern *n.* 型式
alter *v.* 改變	extinct *adj.* 滅絕的	polar *adj.* 極地的
Antarctic *n.* 南極	fossil *adj.* 石化的	predominantly *adv.* 主要的
Arctic *n.* 北極	frequent *adj.* 頻繁的	profitable *adj.* 有利可圖的
chop *n.* 砍	fuel *n.* 燃料	pump *v.* 注入
coal *n.* 煤	habitat *n.* 棲息地	reduce *v.* 減少
consequence *n.* 後果	ice cap *n.* 冰帽	regulation *n.* 法規
consume *v.* 消耗	item *n.* 物品	resource *n.* 資源
consumption *n.* 消耗	melt *v.* 融化	selfish *n.* 自私的
contamination *n.* 污染物	packaging *n.* 包裝	threat *n.* 威脅

環境破壞

地球正承受著極大的壓力，因為人口多達六十億，所以自然資源正在迅速枯竭。各國的湖泊、河川受到污染，樹木也遭到砍伐；工廠製造免洗的商品供人使用，因而將有害的污染物排放到天空；而每天成千上萬的人開車出門，不與他人共乘或是搭乘大眾運輸工具，這也造成額外的污染。雖然人類為了生活，污染就在所難免，可是人們一定要警覺到地球正遭受破壞，希望有了進一步了解後，人們就會付出更多的心力來拯救我們的環境。

全球暖化是指我們地球的平均溫度正逐漸向上攀升，溫度之所以升高，主要是因為我們燃燒煤、石油及其他的石化燃料作為能源，由於氣溫不斷上升，我們目前的天氣型態，可能會在未來產生遽變。假使持續這樣下去，那麼南、北兩極的極地冰帽就會融化，勢必造成海平面上升，引發全世界沿海地區的水患，而全球暖化也代表海水的溫度升高，後果是更頻繁、更強的暴風雨和颶風。

森林是另一個遭受威脅的珍貴資源，樹木與植物產生大量的氧氣，人類才得以呼吸；森林也可以維持土壤的健全，還能幫助大地吸收水分，進而預防水患。可是一旦森林遭到毀壞，許多種類的植物、樹木、昆蟲和動物會失去棲息地，有滅絕之虞。想想我們的森林有多麼重要！砍伐成千上萬的樹木，只為了生產報紙等用過即丟的物品，這似乎很沒有意義。

二十一世紀的我們，都面臨嚴重的環保問題，人們使用和處理資源時，務必更加謹慎；公司團體則要遵守更嚴格的法規，所幸許多公司發現，若遵循環保規範，反而可以省下一筆錢;另一個好現象就是,回收產業的獲利也提高了,只要把用過的產品轉變成新產品就能賺錢。

　　有些國家在環境保護方面立下了很好的典範,拿環保工作以及環保概念來說,德國是全球的翹楚。走進德國的超市,不難發現大多數的物品都沒有什麼包裝;在德國,倒垃圾要付一大筆的費用,因此一般人都致力於垃圾減量,也儘可能做好回收工作。可惜不幸的是,其他國家大部分的人民、公司與政府,對於環境不怎麼懷有敬意,看到這些人一再自私自利、不顧安危地污染地球,真是令人怵目驚心。

人人重環保
世界更美好

環境污染引起的「呼吸困難」

每個人每天平均要吸入一萬公升的空氣，而與空氣接觸的肺泡總面積多達二十五平方公尺；空氣汙染的影響在於呼吸器官的健康會受到破壞。

空氣汙染物的種類眾多，包括：飄塵、二氧化硫、氮氧化物與光化學煙霧、一氧化氮、碳氫化合物和多環芳香。這些空氣汙染物會使人呼吸不適、嘔心、消化不良和暈眩；嚴重時會傷害眼結膜、鼻咽粘膜及呼吸道，引起局部發炎、組織壞死，直接傷害心、肺、神經功能，造成慢性鼻咽炎、慢性支氣管炎、肺纖維化、肺氣腫。有些汙染物經過紫外線照射發生光化學反應後，還有致癌的危險性。

愈都市化的地區，肺癌的發生率也愈高。事實上我們每個人都是空氣汙染的製造者，同時我們每個人也都是空氣汙染的受害者，所以讓大家都深入了解空氣汙染對健康的影響，才能從自身做起，進而防止汙染的危害。

Unit 20 *Rip Van Winkle*

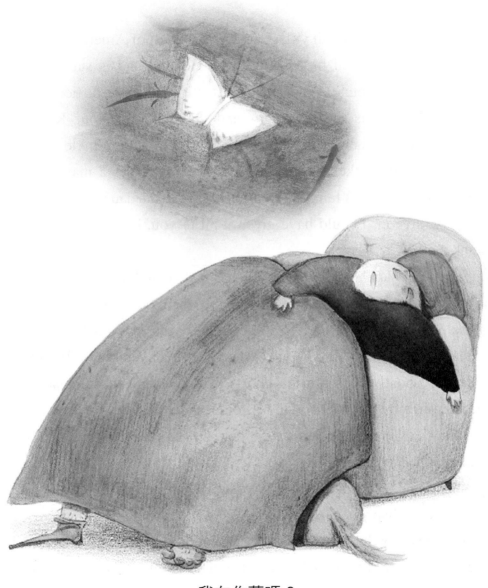

我在作夢嗎？

Rip Van Winkle

"Rip Van Winkle" is perhaps the most famous folk story came out of America. The story was written by a man called Washington Irving who lived from 1783 to 1859. The folk story is a classic because of the symbolism of what happens to the main character, Rip Van Winkle. His story represents what happened to America during the historic period of the American War of Independence. 5

The story begins in a small village on the east coast of America. Rip Van Winkle has recently arrived in America from Holland and is suffering the tough life of a poor colonist. What makes his life even more difficult is his demanding wife who is always angry and complaining about Rip Van Winkle's behavior. To help relieve his pressures, Rip Van Winkle turns to alcohol, but this only makes matters worse and he becomes a man with no great hopes about his or his family's future. He says to his daughter, "You see this village we live in, I could have given it all to you, but over the years I have drank it all away." 10 / 15

One day, Rip Van Winkle decides he has had enough of village life. He gathers up a few possessions and walks deep into the mountains with his dog. During the day, he hunts in the wide open landscapes. At night, he finds a cave and lays down. But before he falls asleep, Rip Van Winkle finds himself surrounded by ghosts. They are the ghosts of old American colonists who have died before him. He listens to their stories and drinks their wine without realizing that the wine contains a magic potion. The magic potion puts Rip Van Winkle into a deep sleep. 20

Rip Van Winkle sleeps for twenty years. When he finally wakes, he is unsure of what had happened, so he decides to walk back to the village. When he returns, he realizes the situation is very different in the village than how it was when he left. He discovers his wife has died and he notices the houses and streets in the village look cleaner, larger and more orderly than before. 25

His daughter recognizes him, cooks him a fine meal and gives him new clothes. But the greatest surprise for Rip Van Winkle concerns his village. 30 During his absence, it has become a part of the United States of America.

The symbolism of Rip Van Winkle represents the ascendance of the United States of America. His old demanding wife represents Britain, the ruler of the colony before independence. Rip Van Winkle represents the thousands of colonists who led very difficult lives when they first arrived 35 from Europe. His return to his home village to start a new life represents the optimism that the Americans felt with the founding of their own country. Rip Van Winkle has been extremely popular both as a book and a play for almost two hundred years. It is an amusing and sanguine folk story and one in which Americans take great pride. 40

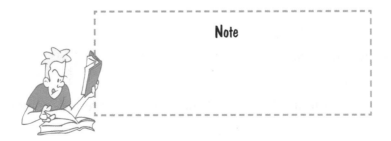

Note

Multiple Choice

—— 1. The story of Rip Van Winkle —————.

    (A) is a true story about the American War of Independence

    (B) is a fictional story that is closely symbolic of the birth of the United States

    (C) is amazing because it is very rare for people to sleep for twenty years

    (D) is a horror story that focuses on the ghosts of old American colonists

—— 2. Washington Irving —————.

    (A) is a friend of Rip Van Winkle

    (B) was born during the period of the American War of Independence

    (C) wrote the popular story "Rip Van Winkle"

    (D) is one of the ghosts of old American colonists in the story

—— 3. Rip Van Winkle was born in —————.

    (A) America but his parents were Dutch

    (B) Holland and moved to America to search for colonists

    (C) Holland and became a European colonist in America

    (D) America and moved to Holland to see his daughter

—— 4. The main character in the story decides to leave the village —————.

    (A) because he wants to go hunting

    (B) to get away from village life

    (C) to search for ghosts who can give inspiration to fight for the United States

    (D) to sleep in the mountain for twenty years

—— 5. Rip Van Winkle doesn't realize he —————.

    (A) is drinking magic potion

    (B) has become a ghost of a former colonist

    (C) has magic powers that will transform America

    (D) represents Britain, the ruler of the colony before independence

—— 6. The magic potion makes Rip Van Winkle ————.

(A) return to his village because he is so tired

(B) become a ghost of a former colonist

(C) realize what has happened to his family and the village

(D) sleep for twenty years without waking

—— 7. The biggest surprise for Rip Van Winkle is that ————.

(A) his village is no longer a British colony

(B) his village still exists despite his twenty-year absence

(C) the United States has become a land of magical symbolism

(D) his daughter still recognizes him

—— 8. The symbolism of the story matches the ————.

(A) early history of the United States of America

(B) way many colonists feel about the countries they finally called home

(C) formation process of most modern countries

(D) relationship between most married couples

—— 9. Rip Van Winkle's wife probably represents ————.

(A) the kind of housewife that most men are afraid of

(B) the ascendance of the United States

(C) Britain, the ruler of the colony before independence

(D) the optimism that the Americans felt with the founding of their own country

—— 10. Americans take pride in the story of Rip Van Winkle ————.

(A) mainly because it is amusing

(B) because it is the most scary story every written

(C) because it can be performed on stage as well as read in a book

(D) because it is an sanguine way to retell the birth of the United States

Try This!

Place a "✓" beside the sentence that uses the key word correctly, and a "✗" to the one that uses wrongly.

colonist

—————— Throughout history, thousands of colonists lived difficult lives in their new countries.

—————— My friend was once a colonist but now he's an accountant.

symbolism

—————— James often tells me how much he enjoys symbolism in art.

—————— Symbolism helped Veronica pass the exam.

wake

—————— I can't wake any longer because I'm so tired from work.

—————— Stay another hour because I'm sure he will wake soon.

character

—————— Delroy got married last year to a character I've never met before.

—————— Each character in the story is amusing in his or her own way.

recognize

—————— Do you recognize the boy in this photograph?

—————— I only recognize him because you said you had a brother.

sanguine

—————— I thought it would be sanguine to mention now that I can't go to your party.

—————— The sanguine story leaves you feeling good about the future.

Key Words

absence *n.* 不在

amusing *adj.* 有趣的

ascendance *n.* 權勢

cave *n.* 洞穴

classic *n.* 經典作品

colonist *n.* 拓殖者

demanding *adj.* 苛求的

folk *adj.* 民間的

found *v.* 建立

Holland 荷蘭

landscape *n.* 地形

optimism *n.* 樂觀

possession *n.* 所有物

potion *n.* 藥劑

relieve *v.* 減輕

sanguine *adj.* 樂觀的

symbolism *n.* 象徵

李伯大夢

　　《李伯大夢》也許是最為世人熟知的美國民間傳說，是由華盛頓・爾文（生於1783年，卒於1859年）所撰寫的。主角李伯・凡・文克的遭遇，因極富象徵性，使得這個民間故事成了經典之作，而他的事蹟也代表了美國獨立戰爭這段歷史中，美國所遭逢的點點滴滴。

　　故事在美國東岸的一個小村莊開場，李伯才剛從荷蘭來到美洲，在這個窮困的殖民地裡生活倍極艱辛，而他的太太又常嫌東嫌西，不但常生氣，還對李伯的行為多所抱怨，讓他的生活更形痛苦。為了減輕壓力，李伯藉酒澆愁，可是這只會讓事情更糟，最後他對自己和家庭的未來也不抱什麼希望，他對女兒說：「妳看看我們住的這個村子，本來我可以把整個村子都交到妳手上，不過這些年，都給我喝酒敗光了。」

　　有一天，李伯再也受不了村裡的生活了，他收拾了幾件物品，帶著狗走進深山，白天在曠野中打獵，到了晚上，他找個洞穴躺下歇息，不過他還沒有睡著，就發現自己的四周都是鬼魂，這些鬼魂是早期來到美洲，且已經作古的殖民者。李伯一邊聽著他們的軼事，一邊喝他們的酒，卻不知這酒帶有神奇的藥性，使得李伯進入沉睡之中。

　　李伯一睡就是二十年，最後終於醒了過來，他也不清楚到底是怎麼一回事，所以打算回村裡瞧一瞧。回去之後，才知道村子裡的情況，已經和他離家時大不相同，他發現他的太太已經死了，也注意到村中的屋舍街道看起來比以前更乾淨寬敞，也更為整齊。他的女兒認出他來，為他煮了一頓大餐，還給他新衣服穿，可是最讓李伯訝異的還是他的村莊。他不在的這段期間，村莊已經成為美國的一部分。

　　李伯象徵美國的主權，而上了年紀又要求嚴苛的太太象徵英國，也就是殖民地獨立之前的統治者。李伯這個角色也代表千千萬萬的殖民者，初次從歐洲來到此地，過著艱苦的生活；他回到自家的村莊重新生活，則象徵美國人建立自己國家時的樂觀態度。《李伯大夢》不僅是家喻戶曉的一本書，也是一齣幾乎有兩百年歷史的劇本，是個既有趣又充滿樂觀的民間故事，美國人深深引以為傲。

作家小檔案

Washington Irving (1783～1859)

Washington Irving 是美國作家，被稱為「美國文學之父」。他從小就在父母的溺愛中長大，不願上大學，只在一家法律事務所斷斷續續地學習法律。年輕時即在報紙上發表一系列怪誕的諷刺雜文，也曾到歐洲和加拿大四處遊歷，他還曾應邀到美國駐西班牙公使館擔任隨員。他的許多作品都深受好評，最偉大的文學成就是《見聞札記》(The Sketch Book of Geoffrey Crayon)。Washington Irving 晚年一直住在紐約州的家中，專心從事文學創作，主要寫傳記作品。

Computer Games

金庸群俠傳、三國志、星海爭霸、太空戰士…
嘿嘿…你是不是也和我一樣愛打電玩呢？

Computer Games

Everywhere people are playing computer games. In fact, computer games are so common that they can now be considered a part of youth culture in most countries of the world. With the press of a few buttons, anyone can drive a racing car, fight off evil gladiators or fly through space on a mission to save the Earth. When you compare these things to doing your homework, it's no wonder that playing computer games is so popular. Everyone has his favorite type of game. Some people like adventure games, where they take a character through mysterious buildings on the search for clues. Other people prefer sports games such as football and tennis. And of course fighting games and science fiction games are always popular.

Computer games were first played in the 1970's. These games were very simple, with few graphics and controls. One of the first games was called "Pong." This was a game for two players that involved two bats and a ball. The object of the game was the same as real-life table tennis. But despite its simplicity, "Pong" became very popular. A few years later, the Atari company made a huge breakthrough. They created a console that allowed people to play classic games like "Space Invaders," "Pacman" and "Frogger" for the first time in their own homes. Since the early days of Atari, game consoles such as "Nintendo," "PlayStation" and "Dreamcast" have kept millions of youngsters entertained for billions of hours. As time goes on, new game consoles are introduced that have far greater power. In fact, the greatest challenge these days is for software designers to create games that can test the limits of the game console power.

Also popular are the games that can be played on a personal computer (PC). In fact, almost every PC sold these days comes with a few simple games like "Solitaire" and "Minesweeper." However, there are thousands of other more sophisticated games for PC owners to play. The best thing about PC games is that they come with all the advantages and functions of a

5

10

15

20

25

computer. For example, PC games can be bought on CD, downloaded on floppy disks or taken off the Internet. You can stay at home and play a game 30 of golf over the Internet against your friend who is sitting in his apartment. Alternatively, you can play a game of Backgammon against someone from Brazil whom you have never met before.

Many of today's games make you feel like you are actually in a fight, in a game of soccer or skiing down a mountain. This effect is known as creating 35 a virtual reality. Some people say computer games of the future will be able to transport the player into games that will be difficult to distinguish from real life. In this sense, computer games may become so realistic that the player may not even know whether he or she is playing a game or not. Those games will make the games of today seem like "Pong." 40

Note

True or False

——(1) Computer games are considered a part of youth culture because they are mostly played by young people.

——(2) It's easier for most students to begin playing a game than to sit down and do their homework.

——(3) Computer games were first played in the 1970's.

——(4) "Pong" was a game that people enjoyed because it was so easy.

——(5) Today there is a much wider choice of game consoles than there was when Atari first appeared.

——(6) Most people want their consoles to have more power because game software is now so advanced.

——(7) PC games are more widely available than console games.

——(8) You can play a game of Backgammon against someone in Germany by playing with a game console.

——(9) To be able to play football on a computer game, the player must be able to play football in real life.

——(10) Because there are already so many games and game consoles available, it is unlikely that games in the future will become more realistic.

> ## Try This!

One day you receive this flyer in the mail. Use it to complete the sentences.

> **Games Superstore**
>
> **For PC and console games**
> **Classic games from the 70's, 80's and 90's**
> **Virtual reality games with sophisticated graphics**
> **Guaranteed lowest prices in Toronto**
> **Trade in your old games for used games**
> **Open Tuesday–Sunday 11 a.m.–10 p.m.**
> **274 Lakes Avenue, Toronto**
> **Or 24 hours a day at www.supergame.ca**

1) The Games Superstore seems to be a good place to buy cheap games because it ——————————— the cheapest games in ——————————.

2) Customers who don't have console may still be interested in the Games Superstore if they own a ——————————— ———————————.

3) The only way to buy a game from the Superstore on Monday is to visit ———————————.

4) If people are bored with their games, they can ——————————— in their old games for other games that other people have previously owned.

5) If you want to play games that are no longer produced, it may be possible to buy them at the ——————————— ———————————.

6) The range of ——————————— ——————————— games are perfect for people who want the best visual imagery currently available.

Key Words

alternatively *adv.* 選擇地	distinguish *v.* 分辨	graphic *n.* 圖片
backgammon *n.* 西洋雙陸棋	evil *adj.* 邪惡的	involve *v.* 包含
bat *n.* 球拍	fiction *n.* 虛構	software *n.* 軟體
clue *n.* 線索	floppy disk *n.* 軟碟片	sophisticated *adj.* 複雜的
console *n.* 主機	gladiator *n.* 鬥士	table tennis *n.* 桌球

電動玩具

　　什麼地方都有人在玩電動玩具，其實現在電玩相當普遍，全世界大多數國家都是如此，可以視為青少年文化的一部分。只要按幾個按鈕，誰都可以開賽車，擊退邪惡的鬥士，或是接獲任務出航太空以拯救地球。拿這些和寫功課一比，也難怪打電動會這麼風行。每個人都有自己最喜歡的遊戲類型，有些人喜歡冒險遊戲，帶著主角穿梭於神秘的建築中尋找線索，有些人比較喜歡體育遊戲，像是足球和網球，當然格鬥遊戲和科幻遊戲也不乏愛好者。

　　電動是1970年代才有的，當時的遊戲很陽春，沒什麼畫面，也沒太多的控制鈕，最早的遊戲當中，有一款叫做「乒乓球大戰」，是兩位選手用兩支拍子、一顆球來比賽，遊戲的主題就跟現實生活中的乒乓球一樣。儘管很陽春，「乒乓球大戰」還是紅透半邊天，幾年之後，Atari公司有了重大的突破，他們研發出一種主機，讓一般人可以在家裡玩遊戲，這些遊戲可說是經典之作，像是「太空侵略者」、「小精靈」、「青蛙過街」等等。從早期的Atari開始，一直到任天堂、PS、DC等遊戲主機，都讓千千萬萬的青少年度過無數的歡樂時光。隨著時代的演進，遊戲主機推陳出新，功能更為強大。事實上，最近軟體設計師最大的挑戰，就是研發出可以超越主機強大功能的遊戲。

　　另外也很風行的，是可以在個人電腦(PC)上玩的遊戲。其實幾乎目前販售的每一臺個人電腦都會附一些簡單的遊戲，像是「接龍」和「踩地雷」等，不過，個人電腦可以玩的，還有其他千百種更為複雜的遊戲。用電腦玩遊戲最棒的地方，在於電腦的優勢和功能在這時候都可以派上用場。比如說，要在個人電腦上玩遊戲，直接買光碟片就可以了，也可以下載到軟碟上，或是從網路上抓下來。你可以待在家中，透過網際網路，和同樣坐在自家公寓的朋友比一場高爾夫球；你也有其他的選擇，比方說和一位素未謀面的巴西人，比一盤西洋雙陸棋。

　　現在很多的遊戲都讓你有如親臨戰場，好像親自參加足球比賽，或者彷彿自己滑雪下山，這種效果就是創造虛擬實境。有人說日後的電玩能將玩家傳送到遊戲中，難以區分遊戲和現實，這麼說來，電玩可以變得十分逼真，甚至到了連玩家都無法分辨自己是否在玩遊戲的地步，而這些遊戲問世之後，就會讓現今的遊戲，變得跟以前的「乒乓球大戰」一樣落伍。

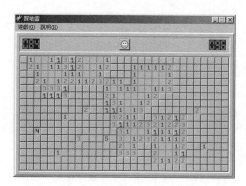

The Story of Elvis Presley

"Before Elvis, there was nothing...But after Elvis, nothing was the same."   —*John Lennon*

The Story of Elvis Presley

Elvis Presley was born on January 8, 1935 in Tupelo, Missouri. When Elvis was young, his family moved around until they eventually settled in Memphis, Tennessee. For the rest of his life, Elvis always called Memphis his home. For his eleventh birthday, Elvis received a US$7.75 guitar from his parents. He was an enthusiastic and confident young man and this led him to   5
enter a singing contest when he was eighteen years old. In the contest Elvis came second. But he wasn't discouraged by not winning, instead, he went straight into a studio to record his two favorite songs.

In 1954, Elvis signed a contract with the Sun Record Company and continued to record songs. The following year, Elvis made his television   10
debut. For the first time people could see his thick black hair, his handsome face and his outrageous dancing style. It was a time when rock'n'roll was starting to spread around America and replace jazz as the most popular music. Songs like "Heartbreak Hotel," "Hound Dog" and "Don't be Cruel" became huge hits in America and the rest of the world. Suddenly, Elvis was a   15
superstar and everywhere he went thousands of teenagers followed him screaming. People began imitating the clothes Elvis wore and even the way he brushed his hair. But the biggest influence Elvis had was with his songs. In the late 1950's, rock'n'roll was accepted as the world's most popular style of music.   20

The image of Elvis became so popular that he began making movies in which he sang many of his lines. In 1957, Elvis bought a pink Cadillac car for his mother and a mansion for himself in Memphis which he called "Graceland." The following year, Elvis was made to serve in the U.S. Army. He joined other regular soldiers in Germany for nearly two years, and when   25
he came out in 1960 he focused on acting and making movies. Many of the movies included songs that went on to become hit records. But in the 1960's, many other rock'n'roll bands became popular and Elvis had to compete with

the musicians he had influenced. One of the bands who admired Elvis was the English band "The Beatles." In 1965, the Beatles met Elvis while they were 30 playing a concert tour in America.

Elvis was married to Priscilla Beaulieu in 1967, a woman he had known since high school. However, the marriage was difficult because Elvis was one of the most famous people in the world. Elvis returned to the stage to perform in the early 1970's but his appearance had changed dramatically. The young 35 handsome Elvis had become overweight and unattractive. In 1973, Elvis and Priscilla divorced, and in the following years Elvis suffered poor health. In August 1977, Elvis died of a heart attack while he was home in his Graceland mansion. People all around the world were shocked when they heard Elvis was dead. For millions of people, Elvis Presley was the voice of rock'n'roll 40 and a major part of their own youth. But Elvis left the world with no doubt that he, who helped change popular music, will remain number one rock'n'roll singer for a very long time.

Note

Multiple Choice

—— 1. Elvis lived his life ————.

    (A) in the city where he was born

    (B) as a jazz superstar

    (C) mainly in Tupelo, Missouri

    (D) in many places but he always considered Memphis his home

—— 2. For his eleventh birthday, Elvis received ————.

    (A) a CD player from his parents

    (B) a guitar from his parents

    (C) a microphone from his best friend

    (D) a CD from his brother

—— 3. Elvis signed a record contract ————.

    (A) after winning a contest when he was young

    (B) with the Sun Record Company after his television debut

    (C) which gave him the chance to record more songs

    (D) which made him rich overnight

—— 4. People saw Elvis on television ————.

    (A) for the first time when he was twenty years old

    (B) and immediately recognized his thick black hair

    (C) but were not impressed because his style was familiar

    (D) and were reminded of the thick black hair of the Beatles

—— 5. The songs Elvis sang helped make rock'n'roll ————.

    (A) a style of music that sounded better than screaming

    (B) almost as popular as jazz

    (C) the most popular form of music in the world

    (D) the noisiest music ever heard

—— 6. Elvis bought a Cadillac car ——————.

    (A) for his personal and family use

    (B) for his mother and a mansion for himself in the late 1950's

    (C) so he could drive his mother to Graceland

    (D) to show off his wealth

—— 7. In the 1960's Elvis was not as popular as ——————.

    (A) he had been in the 1950's despite his fame and influence

    (B) all the English bands that held concerts in America

    (C) he had been before because of the way he spent his money

    (D) he had been in Missouri because of his old age

—— 8. Elvis experienced problems with his marriage because ——————.

    (A) of his bad health in the 1970's

    (B) Priscilla Beaulieu was much too young for him

    (C) of who he was and what he had achieved

    (D) he was a man of violence

—— 9. Elvis returned to the stage to perform in the early 1970's ——————.

    (A) but he had become overweight and unattractive

    (B) and remained the most popular singer at the time

    (C) when he moved into "Graceland" in Memphis

    (D) because he had spent most of his money

—— 10. People were surprised when they heard Elvis was dead because ——————.

    (A) he was not so old

    (B) he was very healthy

    (C) he was part of their youth and the voice of rock'n'roll

    (D) people had thought of Elvis as a superman

Try This!

Match the left with the right.

1) Born on January 8   A) popular

2) In the 1950's, rock'n'roll was...   B) superstar

3) Where Elvis recorded his songs   C) Elvis Presley

4) One of Elvis' songs   D) concert tour

5) What Elvis became   E) studio

6) The Beatles met Elvis during...   F) heart attack

7) What Elvis died of   G) Heartbreak Hotel

Key Words

accept *v.* 接受

appearance *n.* 外表

Cadillac *n.* 凱迪拉克

contract *n.* 合約

debut *n.* 初次登臺

divorce *v.* 離婚

hit *n.* 成功

imitate *v.* 模仿

jazz *n.* 爵士樂

mansion *n.* 宅邸

outrageous *adj.* 驚人的

record *v.* 錄製

rock'n'roll *n.* 搖滾樂

studio *n.* 錄音室

貓王艾維斯‧普里斯萊的故事

1935年一月八日，艾維斯‧普里斯萊出生於密蘇里州的特培洛。艾維斯還小的時候，他家常四處遷移，直到最後才在田納西州的孟斐斯定居，此後一生，艾維斯都說孟斐斯就是他的家鄉。十一歲的生日，艾維斯從父母親那兒收到一把價值七點七五美元的吉他，他是個熱情洋溢又很有自信心的年輕小伙子，十八歲那年參加了一場歌唱比賽，雖然艾維斯這次比賽只得了第二名，未能奪冠，不過他並不灰心，不久就進錄音間錄製了兩首自己最喜愛的歌曲。

1954年，艾維斯與昇陽(Sun)唱片公司簽約，不斷錄製歌曲。接下來那年，艾維斯首次在電視上亮相，這是大家第一次看到他一頭濃密烏黑的頭髮、俊俏的臉龐以及令人嘆為觀止的舞步，當時，搖滾樂正漸漸傳遍全美國，取代爵士樂成為最受歡迎的音樂。「Heartbreak Hotel」、「Hound Dog」、「Don't be Cruel」等歌曲在美國以及世界各地大受歡迎，一時之間，艾維斯成了超級巨星，不管走到哪裡，都有數以千計的青少年緊跟在後，尖叫不斷；大家也模仿起艾維斯的穿著，甚至是他的髮型。而艾維斯最大的影響力還是在於他的歌曲，1950年代末期，大家都認定搖滾樂是當時全世界最普遍的音樂類型。

艾維斯的形象大受歡迎，所以他也開始拍電影，電影裡的許多臺詞，他都是用唱的。1957年，艾維斯買了一輛粉紅色凱迪拉克轎車給母親，也替自己在孟斐斯買了一座名為「恩典之地」的豪宅。第二年，艾維斯受到徵召，進入美軍服役，他和其他的一般兵一樣，到德國將近兩年的時間；1960年退伍後，他把重心放在演戲和拍片上，很多部電影中的歌曲，不久就成了大賣的唱片。不過1960年代，許多曾受到艾維斯影響的搖滾樂團也漸漸受到大眾喜愛，所以艾維斯必須和這些音樂人一同競爭。不少樂團對艾維斯仰慕有加，包括英國的「披頭四」樂團。1965年，披頭四到美國巡迴演唱時，和艾維斯見上一面。

1967年，艾維斯和普莉西拉‧貝洛結婚，是他中學就認識的女子，不過婚姻並不平順，因為艾維斯是舉世知名的人物。1970年代早期，艾維斯重返舞臺，不過他的外表已經大變，原本年輕帥氣的艾維斯，此時卻體重過重，一點吸引力也沒有。1973年，艾維斯和普莉西拉離婚，接下來的幾年，艾維斯一直苦於身體狀況不佳，1977年八月，艾維斯在自家的「恩典之地」豪宅中死於心臟病。聽到艾維斯死去的消息，舉世震驚，對無數人來說，艾維斯‧普里斯萊不僅是搖滾樂的代言人，也是他們年輕時很重要的一部分。艾維斯雖然離開了人世，不過他對於流行音樂的變革很有貢獻，將會長保最佳搖滾歌手的地位。

Unit 23

The Work of Amnesty International

有人權，才有希望！

The Work of Amnesty International

Every year thousands of people are imprisoned, tortured and killed for their political beliefs. This happens because the governments of many countries rely on force and violence to maintain their political control. For example, in 1992 a group of soldiers entered La Cantuta University campus in the city of Lima in Peru. The soldiers took nine students from a classroom   5 as well as their professor. None of these people were ever seen again, they simply disappeared. Amnesty International office in Lima was told about the incident, and then the story was spread to Amnesty International members around the world. In response, the members wrote thousands of letters to the government of Peru and told the media in their own countries about the unfair   10 treatment of the people of Peru. Although these people have not been found, the government of Peru came under the world spotlight for its cruelty because of the work of Amnesty International.

This was a typical case for Amnesty International. The main activity of the organization is to alert its members to human rights abuses and help them   15 to publicize and protest each case. By bringing attention to individual cases and notifying the offending governments, Amnesty International helps to bring about justice and fairness in places where they might not otherwise exist. Amnesty International was founded in 1961 in London, the city that has always been the organization's headquarters. It grew from the hopes of   20 former Spanish, Hungarian and South African political prisoners. These men and women wanted an organization established to take action and promote the concept of human rights. From the beginning, the organization grew quickly and attracted thousands of members around the world. In 1977, Amnesty International won the Nobel Peace Prize for its worldwide   25 promotion of human rights.

Today, Amnesty International has more than a million members in over one hundred and fifty countries. It has approximately eight thousand local

offices that research individual cases and report them to the London
headquarters. The goals of Amnesty International are: to free prisoners   30
detained for their belief or because of their origin, to ensure fair and prompt
trials for all political prisoners, to abolish the death penalty and other cruel
treatment of prisoners, to end political executions and disappearances.
Amnesty International believes that every person should have the freedom of
speech, freedom of movement and choice of religion. The organization is not   35
linked to any government, political thought or religion. However, because it
uncovers so many details about international problems, its research is
sometimes used by other organizations such as the United Nations.

Each year Amnesty International uncovers incidents from almost every
country. Recently, it has investigated cases in Russia, Iraq, Sri Lanka,   40
Indonesia, Australia, China, Mexico and the USA. These investigations show
that although the world may seem peaceful, there are still many human rights
abuses being carried out by governments. Amnesty International relies on its
members for money and help. If you want to contribute to a more peaceful
and safer world, then perhaps you should consider becoming a member of   45
Amnesty International.

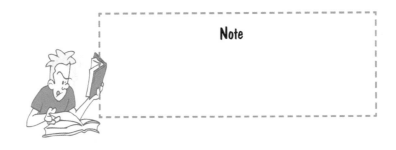

Note

True or False

——(1) Nothing can be done when people receive unfair treatment by governments.

——(2) Many people heard about the professor and the students who were taken by soldiers in Peru.

——(3) Amnesty International helps people by telling them about cruelty in other countries.

——(4) Amnesty International grew from the hopes of former politicians from Spain, Hungary and South Africa.

——(5) Since it was founded in 1961, Amnesty International has been successful even though human rights abuses continue around the world.

——(6) Amnesty International offices always report their cases to the London headquarters.

——(7) Amnesty International has a list of goals that it tries to achieve.

——(8) Amnesty International is not linked to any government nor to the United Nations.

——(9) In reality, human rights abuses only happen in the poorest countries in the world.

——(10) The investigations of Amnesty International remind us the world is not always peaceful and safe.

Try This!

Amnesty International (AI) members often look out for cases where human rights have been abused. Consider the following newspaper headlines and write "AI" beside the ones that you think will interest the members.

———— US President "Not Worried" About Next Election

———— Soldiers Should be Held Responsible for Abusing Their Power

———— Protesters Were Detained During Peaceful Demonstration

———— Earthquake Leaves Thousands of People Homeless

———— Campaign for Human Rights Claims Many Victims

———— Government Official Says No to Tax Cuts

———— Investigation of Former President Will Begin Next Month

———— Technology Stocks Take Another Battering on Wall Street

———— AI Members Alert the United Nations to Unfair Treatment

———— Experts Concerned About Impacts of Global Warming

Key Words

abolish *v.* 廢除	imprison *v.* 監禁	promote *v.* 提倡
abuse *n.* 虐待	investigate *v.* 調查	protest *v.* 抗議
alert *v.* 使警戒	Iraq 伊拉克	publicize *v.* 宣傳
amnesty *n.* 特赦	justice *n.* 正義	spotlight *n.* 注意
detain *v.* 拘留	notify *v.* 宣布	torture *v.* 拷問
execution *n.* 處死	offend *v.* 犯法	treatment *n.* 待遇
force *n.* 武力	penalty *n.* 刑罰	trial *n.* 審判
Hungarian *adj.* 匈牙利的	Peru 秘魯	uncover *v.* 揭露

國際特赦組織的職責

　　每年都有數以千計的人因為政治理念而遭到禁錮、拷打、殺害。會有這種事發生，是因為許多國家的政府都是依恃武力和暴力來鞏固政權，舉例來說，1992年一群士兵進入秘魯利馬市的La Cantuta大學校園，士兵到一個班上，把九名學生連同教授一起帶走，後來就再也沒有看到這些人了，他們就此憑空消失。國際特赦組織位於利馬的辦事處聽說了這件事之後，就把情形轉告國際特赦組織的全球會員，會員寫了數千封的信件向秘魯政府反映，也告訴各自國家的媒體，有一群秘魯的人受到不平等的待遇。雖然這些人尚未找到，不過經由國際特赦組織的行動，秘魯政府卻因其野蠻的行為而受到全世界的檢視。

　　這是國際特赦組織典型的案件，該組織主要的活動就是提醒其下會員留心人權侵犯的問題，也幫助會員公開宣傳每件個案，並加以嚴正抗議。每件個案都受到特別的注意，並將逾越的政府加以公布，如此一來，國際特赦組織就能讓正義公理在各地得以伸張，否則可能會蕩然無存。國際特赦組織於1961年成立於倫敦，一直以來都以這裡為總部的所在地，此組織是出自於早期一些政治犯的希冀，像是西班牙、匈牙利和南非等地的男女政治犯，希望能成立一個組織，採取行動，提倡人權觀念。該組織成立以來成長快速，招募了全世界成千上萬的會員，因為在全球推廣人權，國際特赦組織於1977年榮獲諾貝爾和平獎。

　　而今，國際特赦組織的會員超過一百萬人，來自一百五十多個國家，各地大約有八千個辦事處，調查個別的案件，再向倫敦總部回報。國際特赦組織的宗旨如下：釋放因信仰或是種族之差異而被拘禁的政治犯；確保政治犯儘快得到公平的審判；廢除死刑和其他對犯人不人道的虐待；終止政治上的私刑和「失蹤」。國際特赦組織認為人人都應有言論、遷徙、信仰宗教的自由，該組織和各國政府沒有任何關聯，也不受限於個別的政治思維或信仰。然而，因為常披露國際問題的詳細情形，所以聯合國等組織有時也會援用其研究結果。

　　每年國際特赦組織揭露的事件幾乎遍及各國，近年來調查的案件涵蓋了俄羅斯、伊拉克、斯里蘭卡、印尼、澳洲、中國、墨西哥、美國。這些調查顯示，縱然全世界看似一片祥和，但還是有許多政府進行侵害人權的行為。國際特赦組織靠的是會員的資金與援助，倘若你有意為了全世界的和平安全貢獻一己之力，或許你可以考慮成為國際特赦組織的一員。

國際特赦組織如何採取行動

★在本地新聞媒體宣傳，以引起公眾及目標國政府的注意。

★發出大量的信件、傳真和明信片，直接向目標政府的高級官員申訴。

★遊說本地政府，鼓勵本地當局注意並處理相關事件。

★尋求有影響力的團體和人物，邀請他們為人權運動出一份力。

★舉辦象徵意義的活動，引起其他人的注意，並發動他們的支持。

All the darkness of the world cannot put out the light of one small candle.

整個世界的黑暗掩滅不了一支小燭的光亮。

Unit
24
Thailand

由來已久的泰國，
有其古老且非常獨特的文化喔！

Thailand

Thailand is a country situated in South-East Asia. It's a great country to visit because it offers exotic culture, beautiful scenery and warm temperature. Every year, Thailand receives millions of visitors from all over the world.

The Thai people originally came from two different areas. Some people traveled east from India and others came south from China. These people blended together between the years 100 and 900 A.D. to become a distinct group of people known as the Thai people. Over time the Thais formed villages, and in 1238 they established the first Thai kingdom at a city they called Sukhothai. Many Thais look back on the Sukhothai period as a golden age of the Thai people. The Sukhothai rulers created a new writing script for the Thais and linked the Buddhist religion with Thai culture. The Sukhothai Kingdom remained powerful for about two hundred years before the capital was shifted further south to Ayuthaya because of the threats from Burma.

Ayuthaya became one of the greatest cities in Asia. European traders were welcomed into Thailand during the 1600's and were stunned by the beauty and the size of the city. But again, the capital was moved south to Bangkok in 1769 because of pressure from foreign armies. At this time, European countries were colonizing many countries around the world. Thailand, however, was able to remain independent due to the strong leadership of the Thai Kings and the proud nature of the Thai people.

Today the King of Thailand and the rest of the royal family continue to hold a special position for the Thai people. Recently, many governments have risen and fallen but the royal family has always kept the people united. Buddhism is another part of Thai culture that keeps the people united. Ninety-five percent of the sixty million Thais are Buddhists and it is a religion they take very seriously. Most teenage boys enter the monastery for a period of three to six months between the time they finish school and the time they get married. Altogether there are about 250,000 monks in Thailand, and when you visit the country you will notice their orange robes and shaved heads wherever you go.   30

When many people go to Thailand, they only see the crowded city of Bangkok with all its traffic and pollution. What can compensate the visitor there is excellent shopping in Bangkok, but there are many other great places to visit as well. Chiang Mai in northern Thailand is famous for its temples and is surrounded by mountains. Phuket in southern Thailand has paradise   35 beaches and delicious seafood. There are also hundreds of national parks in Thailand which are great for trekking and camping.

Most Thais these days are still involved in farming, so resources such as rubber, rice and sugar are important for the Thai economy. In recent years, manufacturing has also become widespread, especially around Bangkok.   40 Another major source of income for Thailand is tourism. The Thais realize how vital the tourists are for their economy, and therefore they try to make all visitors feel welcome. So when you go to Thailand, get ready to receive many friendly smiles. And make sure when you receive one you give your best smile in return.   45

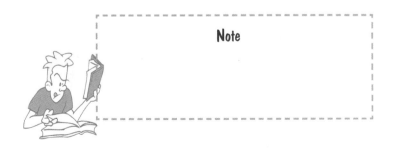

Note

Multiple Choice

—— 1. Millions of people visit Thailand ————.

    (A) because it is a country that has many man-made attractions

    (B) but most prefer not to return

    (C) to experience the way of life of those who take their religion seriously

    (D) to be monks or nuns for several months

—— 2. The Thai people originally ————.

    (A) believed in Buddhism and lived in temples

    (B) came from India and China

    (C) came from Indonesia and Burma

    (D) lived upon manufacturing

—— 3. Sukhothai was the Thai Kingdom that ————.

    (A) came after the others in India and China

    (B) many Thai people take most pride in

    (C) became famous for its foreign influences

    (D) remained powerful for about one hundred years

—— 4. The Sukhothai period had an influence on Thai culture ————.

    (A) which can still be felt today

    (B) because of the links the rulers had with the Burmese

    (C) that lasted for approximately two hundred years

    (D) mainly because Sukhothai was once the capital of Thailand

—— 5. The Thai capital was forced to move south on two occasions ————.

    (A) but it refused to do so

    (B) because it was warmer in the south

    (C) and in the near future it will probably do so again

    (D) because of the threats from foreign armies

—— 6. During the period of European colonization, Thailand was able to remain independent ————.

(A) because of the strong leadership of the Thai Kings

(B) because Europeans respected the peaceful nature of Buddhism

(C) and compete with strong European countries

(D) and make the nearby countries its colonies

—— 7. The Thai people respect the royal family ————.

(A) instead of finding personal strength through religion

(B) except when they rise or fall

(C) because the Kings have been successful in keeping the people united

(D) because they are taught to do so since childhood

—— 8. Buddhism in Thailand ————.

(A) is only practiced by monks who shave their hair and wear orange robes

(B) is widespread throughout the country and respected by most people

(C) is not at all different from Buddhism in China or India

(D) is the only religion exist in Thailand

—— 9. Bangkok is ————.

(A) a city of temples surrounded by mountains and paradise beaches

(B) the capital of Thailand which features excellent shopping and light traffic

(C) the capital of Thailand crowded with people and cars

(D) the place where the Sukhothai Kingdom was established

—— 10. Tourism is one of the most important sources of income ————.

(A) because the Thais are too lazy to work in the factory

(B) because not as many foreigners visit Thailand as they once did

(C) because the Thais are not as rich as they were in their golden age

(D) for Thailand and this is partly why the Thais are so friendly to visitors

Try This!

The following is a list of what has been or currently is in Thailand. Mark the correct column for each item.

	Thai Culture	Thai Place	Foreign Influence
Sukhothai			
Chinese Culture			
Thai Buddhism			
Chiang Mai			
Phuket			
Inward Tourism			
King of Thailand			
Thai Script			
Burmese Armies			
Bangkok			
Thai Food			
Indian Culture			
Ayuthaya			

Key Words

Bangkok 曼谷
blend *v.* 融合
Buddhism *n.* 佛教
Buddhist *n.* 佛教徒
Burma 緬甸
colonize *v.* 殖民

compensate *v.* 補償
distinct *adj.* 獨特的
exotic *adj.* 外來的
monastery *n.* 僧院
monk *n.* 和尚
robe *n.* 長袍

situate *v.* 位於
stun *v.* 嚇呆
temple *n.* 寺廟
Thailand 泰國
tourism *n.* 觀光業
trek *v.* 健行

泰國

　　泰國是位於東南亞的國家，文化極富異國風情，而且風景秀麗，氣候暖和，是觀光的絕佳去處，每年泰國都迎接了幾百萬來自世界各地的觀光客。

　　泰國人起源於兩個不同的地域，有些人從印度東來，還有一些人從中國南下，這些人在西元100年到900年間融合在一起，成為獨特的一群人，也就是泰民族。久而久之，泰國人建立起村落，並於1238年在他們所稱的素可泰城，建立了第一個泰國王朝，許多泰人回顧素可泰時期，都認為這是泰民族的黃金時代，素可泰的國王為泰人創制一套新式的書寫文字，並將佛教和泰國文化緊扣在一起。素可泰王朝強盛了將近兩百年之後，卻因為來自緬甸的威脅，只好將首都南移到阿猶他亞。

　　阿猶他亞成了當時亞洲的大都城，西元1600年間，泰國歡迎歐洲商人前來，他們看到該城景色之美、腹地之大，莫不瞠目結舌。可是1769年，受到外國軍隊的威逼，首都再次南遷至曼谷，此時歐洲各國在世界各地許多國家殖民，可是泰國卻因為泰國君王領導有方，加上泰國人自尊心很強，因此得以保持獨立。

　　而今泰國的君王和其他的王室成員，在泰國人的心目中依舊保有其特殊的地位。近年來泰國的政府起起落落，不過泰國王室一直是維繫人民團結的力量，佛教也是泰國文化中維持人民團結的另一支力量，六千萬泰人中，有百分之九十五是佛教徒，而且他們皆以嚴肅的態度看待這個宗教，大多數十來歲的小男孩在學成之後到結婚之前，都要到寺廟裡待上三到六個月的時間。泰國一共有二十五萬的僧侶，到該國參觀，不管你走到哪裡，都會看到他們穿著橘色僧袍，頭髮都已經剃除。

　　很多人到了泰國，只看到曼谷擁擠的市容，交通混亂，污染嚴重，不過在曼谷購物非常棒，算是對觀光客的一種補償，但是除了曼谷外，還有許多好地方可以參觀。泰國北部的清邁以寺廟聞名，處於群山環抱之中；泰國南部的普吉島擁有海濱樂園以及美味的海產；泰國還有好幾百個國家公園，很適合健行和露營。

　　時下大多數的泰人仍然務農,所以橡膠、稻米、糖等資源對於泰國的經濟十分重要,近年來製造業也漸趨普及,以曼谷周邊為最;泰國另一項主要的收入來源就是觀光業,泰國人也深知觀光客攸關他們的經濟,因此他們致力使每位觀光客感到倍受歡迎。所以到了泰國,要準備好面對許多善意的微笑,也請你報以最燦爛的笑顏。

The European Union

你聽過「歐洲聯盟」嗎？
你知道「歐元」能讓你暢行歐洲大大小小的購物中心嗎？

The European Union

If you drive a car from Germany to France, you might not notice you are entering a new country. That's because there are no longer border controls or passport checks between countries as there were years ago. Instead, you might only see a blue flag with twelve gold stars: the flag of the European Union (EU). In fact, this is the way it is now across most of Europe. It is like   5 one large country with different provinces. Altogether there are fifteen European countries connected in the EU. The member countries are Austria, Belgium, Denmark, Finland, France, Germany, Greece, Ireland, Italy, Luxemburg, the Netherlands, Portugal, Spain, Sweden and the United Kingdom.   10

It is logical to have the European countries united in this way. History tells us that for hundreds of years wars have been fought for the control of Europe. After the devastating world wars of the twentieth century, it became clear that a new way was needed to keep peace. The result is an integrated Europe, both economically and politically. Integration has advantages, such   15 as making Europe competitive with the other world powers. Individually, the European countries knew they were too small to compete with the USA, Russia and China. But when the fifteen countries are united in the EU, they have a population of more than three hundred and seventy million people. This means real economic and political power.   20

Every year the member countries of the EU are getting closer and closer. In the 1990's, the border controls between each country came down, and now eleven of the EU countries share the same currency known as the "Euro." Some people say the speed at which Europe has integrated has been too fast. They say there isn't enough trust between the countries because only half a   25 century ago most of the EU countries were involved on opposite sides of a world war. They also argue that the huge cultural and historical differences that exist between member countries will never allow the EU to fully

cooperate politically. These people are called "Euro Skeptics" because of their skeptical attitudes. The United Kingdom in particular remains skeptical   30
about participating in a deeper integration. In 1994, the United Kingdom decided not to join the other members in the currency union although it kept its membership of the EU.

Other people are optimistic about the concept of the EU. They say the benefits of having a single currency and no border controls will make the EU   35
as economically powerful as the USA. Indeed for people who hold a European passport the benefits are great. For example, a student from Portugal can study in Sweden without any problems and an Austrian woman can reside and work in France for the rest of her life if she wants. This movement and migration of people within the EU is rapidly changing the face   40
of Europe. But only time will tell if the concept is successful and if the people of Europe are willing and able to integrate completely.

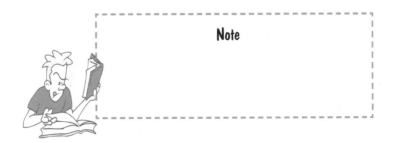

Note

Multiple Choice

—— 1. The European Union appears to ————.

    (A) have changed the political environment in Europe

    (B) allow easier transportation for vehicles and provinces

    (C) be working mainly for people who own their own means of transportation

    (D) unite the currency of all European countries

—— 2. The flag of the European Union ————.

    (A) is red and has ten white stars on it

    (B) is blue and has twelve gold stars on it

    (C) is green and has ten white stars on it

    (D) is brown and has twelve gold stars on it

—— 3. The individual member countries of the EU ————.

    (A) are similar to provinces in the way they cooperate with each other

    (B) believe the old border controls are still necessary for every crossing

    (C) have nothing to gain from other member or non-member countries

    (D) are more powerful in military force than other non-member countries

—— 4. A major advantage of the EU ————.

    (A) is the combined wealth of over three hundred and seventy million people

    (B) is the fact that economic growth is too optimistic to be real

    (C) is the fact that it allows people to reside anywhere in the world

    (D) is the fact that the cultural differences will be diminished in the near future

—— 5. The EU is changing from year to year ————.

    (A) mainly because of the skeptical attitudes of all of its members

    (B) in an official way but not in unofficial ways

    (C) partly because it is becoming more closely integrated

    (D) which makes itself weaker and weaker in world status

—— 6. Some people believe ————.

    (A) that the EU will soon be able to modify the speed of its border controls

    (B) that Europe should not attempt to integrate too quickly

    (C) that the whole world belongs to a union which is different from the EU

    (D) that the EU will be able to defeat America in the coming World War III

—— 7. Euro Skeptics think that ————.

    (A) there is enough trust between European countries

    (B) the "Euro" will ruin the European economy

    (C) huge cultural and historical differences will never allow the EU to fully cooperate politically

    (D) the EU will fail because there are too many member countries

—— 8. The United Kingdom is generally ————.

    (A) unwilling to agree on any decisions made by "Euro Skeptics"

    (B) very pleased with its decision to join the currency union in 1994

    (C) regarded as the head of the other member countries

    (D) considered to be skeptical of the EU despite being a member

—— 9. There are many people who are optimistic ————.

    (A) about the cultural and historical integration of European countries

    (B) about history repeating itself with the new political environment in Europe

    (C) about politics but skeptical about the members who do not want to join

    (D) about the future of Europe and the way the EU works

—— 10. An EU passport ————.

    (A) is more powerful now than it was in the 1950's

    (B) can be issued to non-Europeans

    (C) allows people to live in Portugal but not in Ireland

    (D) allows residents of member countries to live anywhere in the EU

Try This!

The recent formation of the European Union (EU) has had real influences on the way people live. Look at the various issues and mark what the EU has had an influence on.

Influenced by the EU	European	Same as before the EU
	border controls	
	languages	
	money system	
	international trade	
	country leadership	
	jobs and work	
	cultural differences	
	geography	
	population size	
	population spread	
	European cooperation	

Key Words

Austria 奧地利	integrated *adj.* 整合的	Portugal 葡萄牙
Belgium 比利時	integration *n.* 整合	province *n.* 省
border *n.* 邊境	Luxemburg 盧森堡	reside *v.* 居住
cooperate *v.* 合作	Netherlands 荷蘭	skeptic *n.* 懷疑者
currency *n.* 貨幣	participate *v.* 參與	skeptical *adj.* 懷疑的
devastating *adj.* 毀滅性的	passport *n.* 護照	Sweden 瑞典

歐洲聯盟

假使從德國開車到了法國，你可能不會察覺已經到了另一個國家，因為幾年前還有的邊境管制、護照檢查，現在都沒有了。取而代之的，可能是一面有十二顆金色星星的藍色旗幟，這是歐洲聯盟(EU)的旗幟。事實上，現在通行歐洲大多地方的就是這套作法，就好像一個龐大的國家之下，有不同的省份。總計有十五個國家統合在歐盟之下，成員國包括奧地利、比利時、丹麥、芬蘭、法國、德國、希臘、愛爾蘭、義大利、盧森堡、荷蘭、葡萄牙、西班牙、瑞典以及英國。

歐洲各國以此方式結合也不無道理，歷史告訴我們，數百年來，為了稱霸歐洲而導致戰火擾攘，經過二十世紀兩次慘烈的世界大戰之後，維持和平的新方式顯然有其必要，而今天的成果就是經濟和政治雙雙整合後的歐洲。整合有其優點，比方說歐洲因此更有能力與世界強國競爭；若憑一己之力，歐洲各國都了解他們太小了，很難跟美國、俄羅斯、中國匹敵。不過，一旦十五個國家統合在歐盟之下，人口則超過三億七千萬，這股政經勢力不容小覷。

歐盟各成員國之間的關係一年比一年緊密。1990年代，各國之間的邊境管制鬆綁，而今，十一個成員國通用「歐元」這種統一的貨幣；不過部分人覺得歐洲統合的步調操之過急，他們認為國與國之間的互信不足，因為就在半個世紀前，歐盟大多數的成員國都捲入世界大戰的敵對陣營中，這些人還以各成員國之間有著極大的文化和歷史差異為例，證明歐盟不可能在政治上完全整合。正因為這些人所抱持的懷疑態度，他們被稱為「歐元懷疑論者」，特別是英國對於參與更深入的統合還存有疑問。1994年，英國雖然保留歐盟的成員國身分，卻決議不跟從其他成員國加入貨幣聯盟。

其餘的人倒是對歐盟的構想相當樂觀，認為單一貨幣加上取消邊境管制所帶來的好處，能使歐盟在經濟上和美國一樣強大。的確，對於持有歐洲護照的人來說實在好處多多，舉例來說，葡萄牙的學生可以到瑞典唸書，暢行無阻；奧地利的婦女若有意願，那下半生也可以在法國定居、工作。歐盟之內，人民的移動和遷徙正快速改變歐洲的樣貌，不過只有時間能說明這個構想是否能成功，還有歐洲人是否樂意、是否適合進行全面的統合。

Claude Monet and the Impressionists

Waterlilies

就讓莫內帶你走進印象派的世界⋯

Claude Monet and the Impressionists

The French Impressionist painters of the 1870's are famous for being among the greatest innovators of western art. Instead of painting in a photographic style, the Impressionists painted in an imprecise way. Their use of colors and quick brush strokes made the objects in their paintings blend into the background or the foreground. Shapes were no longer hard edged, 5 they were painted as flowing. This was the style that became known as Impressionism. A definition of Impressionism is difficult to make because so many styles and artists were involved in the movement. The style, however, is probably best understood by examining the work of Claude Monet, the Impressionist leader. 10

Claude Monet was born in 1840 and grew up in the West Coast French town of Le Havre. As a teenager, he worked as a caricature artist in his home town. He was a self-confident and determined young man, and the characteristics stayed with him through his entire life. When he was twenty years old, he moved to Paris to study art and this is where he met other young 15 painters with similar ideas. Monet and his artist friends disliked the conventional art styles and became determined to challenge the normal standards. But because their style was innovative, there was no way these artists could sell their work. Monet and his friends were forced to live in poverty throughout the 1860's and 1870's, having to borrow money from 20 relatives and other people.

The 1870's has been called the decade of "Pure Impressionism." It was the decade when the style was new and highly innovative. In 1874 the group held an exhibition of their work in Paris. One of Monet's paintings at this exhibition had the title "Impression: Sunrise." An art critic wrote about the 25 exhibition and called the group "The Impressionists" after the name of this painting and that is how the artists came to be known. Other Impressionist painters included Renoir, Sisley, Pissarro and Bazille. Gradually, Monet and

the other Impressionists started to gain wider recognition of their style. An Impressionist exhibition held in New York in 1886 was very successful and   30
confirmed their reputations. Monet was finally able to sell his paintings and live a more secure lifestyle. In 1883 he bought a house with a large garden in a town west of Paris called Giverny.

While living at Giverny, Monet created a massive water garden which employed six full time gardeners. The water garden was created by Monet as   35
a paradise of color and nature that he could paint over the next twenty-five years. Colors were always essential to Monet's work and during the 1890's he developed a further fascination with the effects of light. Monet traveled and painted around France and other countries in Europe, but he always returned to Giverny to be with his family and the water garden. Claude Monet   40
died in 1926 at the age of eighty-six. By the time of his death, he was world-famous and his paintings were extremely valuable. Monet was a prolific painter and today his masterpieces and those of the other Impressionists can be seen in the best art galleries and private collections around the world.   45

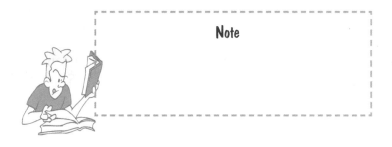

Note

True or False

—(1) The Impressionists were innovative because they painted in a style that hadn't been seen before.

—(2) Instead of painting in a imprecise way, the Impressionists liked to paint in a photographic style.

—(3) One of the reasons Claude Monet is famous is because he was the leader of the Impressionist painters.

—(4) Monet was an Impressionist from the very beginning of his painting career.

—(5) Monet couldn't sell his Impressionist paintings at first because he disliked conventional art.

—(6) An art critic was responsible for the group becoming known as the Impressionists.

—(7) "The Impressionists" is related to the name of one of Monet's paintings, "Waterlilies."

—(8) In 1886 the Impressionists held a successful exhibition of their art in America.

—(9) Colors were important for Impressionists and this is partly the reason why Monet created a massive water garden.

—(10) Monet's paintings are valuable today because they can be seen in private collections.

Try This!

Find words in the article about Claude Monet and the Impressionists which mean the opposite to the following.

From lines 1–21

eastern   _____

precise   _____

slow   _____

background   _____

soft   _____

easy   _____

worst   _____

elderly   _____

different   _____

purchase   _____

From lines 22–45

repetitive   _____

afterwards   _____

quickly   _____

lesser   _____

unsuccessful   _____

questioned   _____

initially   _____

die   _____

insecure   _____

sold   _____

Key Words

caricature *n.* 諷刺漫畫
confirm *v.* 鞏固
conventional *adj.* 傳統的
critic *n.* 評論家
decade *n.* 十年
edge *v.* 使銳利

exhibition *n.* 展覽
fascination *n.* 著迷
gallery *n.* 美術館
imprecise *adj.* 含糊的
impressionist *n.* 印象派畫家
innovative *adj.* 革新的

innovator *n.* 革新者
massive *adj.* 宏偉的
masterpiece *n.* 代表作
photographic *adj.* 寫實的
prolific *adj.* 多產的
stroke *n.* 筆劃

莫內與印象派畫家

1870年代的法國印象派畫家，其大膽創新在西洋美術史上是出了名的，他們一改寫實的畫風，以模糊的畫法取而代之。在他們的用色和迅速的刷筆之下，畫中的物體融入背景或是前景之中，輪廓有如行雲流水，不再有稜有角，這就是有名的印象派風格。因為牽涉到太多的畫風和畫家，所以很難給印象派下個定義，不過，分析印象派大師——莫內的作品，應該就能掌握該派的畫風。

莫內生於西元1840年，在法國西岸的哈佛爾長大。十多歲的時候，在家以畫諷刺漫畫為業，當時他就是個自信堅毅的年輕人，這些特質終生沒有改變。二十歲那年，他搬到巴黎學習藝術，在那裡遇到其他志同道合的年輕畫家，莫內和這些藝術家朋友都不喜歡傳統美術風格，決心要對抗原有的標準。然而，由於畫風過於創新，這群藝術家的畫作都賣不出去，所以1860、1870年代，莫內和朋友們只好過著貧窮潦倒的生活，還得向親戚朋友借錢。

1870年代稱做「純印象派」的十年，這十年間，該畫風才剛出現，富有極高的革新意味。1874年，這群人在巴黎舉辦了一次作品展，其中有一幅莫內的畫，標題為《日出·印象》，有個藝評家寫了展覽觀後感，就以這幅畫的標題統稱這群人為「印象派畫家」，這就是這群藝術家闖出名號的經過。其他的印象派畫家包括雷諾瓦、西斯萊、畢沙羅、巴吉爾等人，莫內與其他的印象派畫家的畫風，逐步獲得更廣大的認同。1886年，印象派在紐約的展出結果相當成功，奠定了他們的名聲，莫內終於可以賣出畫作了，生活也較為安定。1883年，他在巴黎西部的吉維尼鎮買了一棟房子，裡頭有一座大花園。

在吉維尼生活的期間，莫內打造了一座宏偉的水上花園，雇請了六名專任的園丁，莫內將水上花園打造成色彩繽紛的自然樂園，其後的二十五年，他都可以在此盡情作畫。色彩對莫內的作品來說非常重要，1890年代，他又醉心於光線的效果。

莫內一邊旅行，一邊作畫，遊遍了法國與歐洲其他國家，不過他一定會回到吉維尼和水上花園，和家人聚一聚。莫內卒於1926年，享年八十六歲，過世的時候，他已是舉世知名的人物，畫作相當名貴。莫內是個多產的畫家，他的傑作還有其他印象派畫家的代表作，在全世界最好的美術館或是私人收藏中，至今都還可以一睹風采。

穿和服的女人（莫內夫人）
1875～1867年
油畫畫布　231×142cm
美國波士頓美術館館藏

莫內
攝於1901年，時年61歲

日出・印象
1872年
油畫畫布　48×63cm
瑪摩丹美術館館藏

吉維尼的麥草堆
1884年
油畫畫布　65×81cm
日本私人收藏

The Sixties Generation

We are baby boomers!

The Sixties Generation

The twentieth century was a time of extremes, a time of technological breakthrough, of violent world war and of lasting peace and prosperity. One of the greatest extremes occurred in the 1960's. This was the time when the flower people took over world culture. If we look back at that time and compare it with the society today, we can easily see how the influence of the sixties generation changed the way people think.

There are a number of reasons why the sixties were unique. Perhaps the main reason was because it occurred one generation after the bloodiest war in history. The Second World War involved almost every country on earth, several million people were killed and thousands of cities and towns were destroyed. When peace was declared in 1945, the soldiers who fought in the war returned home and people were able to make a fresh start to life. The result was the greatest baby boom the world had ever seen. Between 1945 and 1952, hundreds of millions of babies were born, and ever since this group of people have moved through society together. In the mid-sixties these people, often called the "baby boomers," were at university and learning about the violence of their parents' generation. The huge numbers of people reacting to the horror of war created the peaceful mood of the sixties.

The sixties was a time of experimentation and open-mindedness. In the USA, Scott McKenzie sang, "If you're going to San Francisco, make sure you wear a flower in your hair." Other American musicians who expressed the mood of the sixties included Bob Dylan and Janis Joplin. In the UK and Europe, pop music was equally expressive. The English band "the Beatles" led the way with a long list of hit songs about love. In 1968, at the height of the sixties generation, the Beatles sang their legendary song, "All You Need is Love," to a worldwide television audience of millions. Meanwhile in Paris, university students brought the French city to a standstill with protests against the policies of the French Government. Similar protests occurred in Germany,

5

10

15

20

25

the USA and Australia.

Most of all, people just wanted a peaceful world in which to live and   30
raise their children. The symbols of peace were flowers and living naturally.
Many men at the time grew beards, and long hair for both men and women
was the sixties fashion. Men wore flared trousers and women wore bright
colorful dresses. Many people refused to eat meat and became vegetarians.
Other people left the cities and began living and working in groups where   35
they could live peacefully with each other in the midst of nature.

Reflecting on the sixties, we see that many of the ideas that were
initiated back then are of vital concern today. Environmental awareness, for
example, got its start during the sixties and today it remains a major issue for
governments and protest groups. Gender and racial equality were also   40
debated frequently. Certainly these issues wouldn't be as important as they
are now if these movements hadn't been started in the sixties.

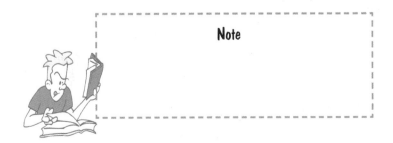

Note

Multiple Choice

—— 1. Baby boomers ——————.

    (A) were born during the sixties

    (B) had graduated from university in the mid-sixties and become powerful in political field

    (C) were those who had babies during the sixties

    (D) were mostly born between 1945 and 1952

—— 2. The sixties generation ——————.

    (A) changed the world because they influenced the way people think today

    (B) were similar to the eighties generation but not any other generation

    (C) were responsible for the birth of the baby boomers

    (D) always wore a flower in their hair

—— 3. The Second World War made people want to live a ——————.

    (A) lifestyle that did not involve making big decisions

    (B) lifestyle that did not differentiate between men and women in any way

    (C) more peaceful life

    (D) more violent life

—— 4. The baby boomers were the most influential people ——————.

    (A) towards the end of the Second World War

    (B) during the sixties partly because they made up much of the population

    (C) during the sixties because they held top positions of power at the time

    (D) during the sixties because they were so fashionable

—— 5. People tried things in the sixties ——————.

    (A) that had never been tried before

    (B) that people today refuse to acknowledge

    (C) because it is argued that they were more intelligent than the current generation

    (D) in traditional but efficient ways

——— 6. Music was important for the sixties generation ————.

    (A) because it was the first time musicians were able to express themselves properly

    (B) because it could help to overcome the hunger for meat

    (C) but since then music has played a lesser role in entertainment

    (D) as a way of communicating their message of love

——— 7. Peace was important for the baby boomers ————.

    (A) because they were shocked at the violence of their parents' generation

    (B) but not as important as other issues such as fashion

    (C) who did not want to struggle for the issues they believed in

    (D) because they deeply believed in Christianity

——— 8. The symbols of peace in the sixties were ————.

    (A) blue jeans and long beards

    (B) the legendary songs sung by the Beatles

    (C) flared trousers and colorful dresses

    (D) flowers and living naturally

——— 9. Radical fashions and alternative lifestyles ————.

    (A) were more common in the sixties than at any other time in recent history

    (B) were embraced by every single person who was alive in the sixties

    (C) have always been popular because people have always believed in equality

    (D) are the symbols of justice in the sixties

——— 10. The sixties was a time when many people debated the ————.

    (A) inequalities found in society

    (B) importance of wearing flared trousers

    (C) rights of all people to destroy the environment

    (D) the choice of eating vegetable or meat

Try This!

Place a "✓" next to what you would expect to have happened in the sixties and a "✗" next to what you don't think would have happened.

—— Mandy goes to the rainbow café and orders a carrot and potato pie.

—— Ian gets a short haircut every six weeks.

—— A family watches a television program about how life was in the sixties.

—— A group of friends sit in a park playing Janis Joplin's songs on guitar.

—— This year's fashionable colors are black, gray and white.

—— People leave their jobs and start a new life in San Francisco.

—— Electronic music without voices is played on the radio.

—— Students say there is nothing they can do about environmental damage.

—— University students protest against racism and gender discrimination.

—— Larry decides not to shave off his beard before his job interview.

—— An office worker downloads information about her holiday destination.

—— Most fashion shops are selling brightly colored clothes.

Key Words

baby boom *n.* 嬰兒潮

beard *n.* 鬍子

bloody *adj.* 血腥的

debate *v.* 爭論

declare *v.* 宣布

experimentation *n.* 實驗

expressive *adj.* 表達的

fashion *n.* 時尚

flare *v.* 向外展開

gender *n.* 性別

generation *n.* 世代

horror *n.* 恐怖

initiate *v.* 發起

legendary *adj.* 傳奇的

mood *n.* 氣氛

prosperity *n.* 繁榮

protest *v.* 反對

racial *adj.* 種族的

react *v.* 反應

refuse *v.* 拒絕

standstill *n.* 停頓

trousers *n.* 褲子

vegetarian *n.* 素食者

六〇年的世代

　　二十世紀是充滿極端的時代，是科技突破的時代，是世界大戰慘烈的時代，也是長久和平繁榮的時代。這麼多極端當中，有一回就發生在1960年代，也就是花樣男女掌控全球文化的年代。回顧彼時，再與今日的社會相比，很容易就看出來，六〇年代那輩人對於人類思想的轉變，有很大的影響力。

　　六〇年代之所以獨特，有許多因素，或許主要原因恰好是在史上最血腥的戰爭之後的第一代。第二次世界大戰，幾乎每個國家都難以倖免，成千上萬的人民遭到殺害，數以千計的都市、城鎮遭到毀壞。1945年宣布和平到來後，作戰的軍人返回家鄉，得以從頭開始新生活，結果造成全球有史以來最大的嬰兒潮，1945年到1952年間，數億名嬰兒誕生，之後，這群人又一起踏入社會。六〇年代中期，俗稱「嬰兒潮世代」的這些人正好上大學，了解他們父母那一輩的慘烈戰事，這一大批人反映出對戰爭的恐懼，進而造成了六〇年代的和平氣象。

　　六〇年代也是實驗與接納新思想的年代。在美國，史考特・麥肯錫唱了一曲「假如你正好要去舊金山，頭上一定要帶朵花」；美國其他的音樂家也表達了六〇年代的氣氛，包括巴布・迪倫、珍妮絲・賈普琳等人。在英國與歐洲，流行樂的表達力可說是有過之而無不及，英國的「披頭四」樂團獨占鰲頭，他們關於愛情的暢銷歌曲可以列出一長串。1968年，正值六〇年代那一輩人的全盛時期，披頭四對全球數百萬電視機前面的觀眾，唱出一首傳奇歌曲——All You Need is Love；同一時期在巴黎，大學生強烈反對法國政府的政策，讓巴黎市完全停擺，而類似的抗議也出現在德國、美國和澳洲。

　　一般人最想要的，不過是個和平的世界，可以生活，可以養育子女，而和平的象徵就是花朵以及順應自然的生活。在當時很多男人蓄鬍子，而且男人女人都留長髮，這就是六〇年代的風尚；男人穿喇叭褲，女人穿鮮豔多彩的服裝，許多人不願意吃肉，成了素食者；其他人遠離城市，一群人一起工作生活，在大自然之中彼此和睦相處。

　　仔細思索六〇年代，看得出當時發起的許多想法，今日仍受到高度重視。舉例來說，環保意識肇始於六〇年代，到了今天，依舊是政府與反對團體的重大議題；兩性平權與種族平等在當時也常有爭論。要不是早在六〇年就推行這些運動，這些議題絕對不會像現今這樣受到重視。

Unit

28 *Animated Films*

主人，我能為您效勞嗎？

叫阿拉丁快點來見我！

Animated Films

Animated films, sometimes called "cartoon films," have been popular for more than sixty years. And when most people think about animated films, they usually think about Disney. That's because Disney has been the most original and innovative maker of animated films. The first feature-length animated film was released in 1937 and was called "Snow White and the Seven Dwarfs." At the time of its release, the other production companies in Hollywood believed a cartoon film would fail. But their doubts were proved unfounded and "Snow White and the Seven Dwarfs" went on to become hugely popular with worldwide audiences. In 1940, Disney followed up with "Pinocchio," and ever since Disney Film Studios have released a great number of films. Some of their most famous films have included "Sleeping Beauty" from 1959 and "Winnie the Pooh" from 1977.

During the 1990's a great revival in Disney animated films occurred. Many people in the industry credit this success to a new group of artists who joined Disney Film Studios in the late 1980's. The leader of the group was Jeffrey Katzenberg, and under his direction Disney produced a number of blockbusters. Films such as "Beauty and the Beast" from 1991 used groundbreaking computer graphics that thrilled audiences around the world. Their follow up film, "Aladdin," earned US$217 million at the box office to make it the most profitable animated film ever. That record was broken by Katzenberg and his team in 1994 with "The Lion King." In fact, "The Lion King" remains the most profitable animated film with an incredible US$313 million taking.

Other Hollywood production studios decided to try their luck with animation. Warner Brothers made "Who Framed Roger Rabbit?" and followed up with "Space Jam," a film which blended animation with basketball legend, Michael Jordan. Then there was a major change in the industry. Jeffrey Katzenberg left Disney and set up a new company in partnership with the influential director Steven Spielberg and music producer David Geffen. The new company was called "DreamWorks" and their first film was called "The Prince of Egypt." Hollywood was shocked because Katzenberg created such a new style of animated film. It was a film made more for adults than for children. "The Prince of Egypt" took four years to make and cost approximately US$100 million. DreamWorks employed 425 artists for the film and consulted approximately five hundred religious leaders and experts. The story was taken directly from the Bible, and this made it a difficult film to make without offending people. Disney continued to make animated films using their proven formula. "Toy Story," "Toy Story 2" and "Tarzan" were great films that enjoyed box office success. In response, DreamWorks produced "Antz" in 1998 and "Chicken Run" in 2000.

Now that Disney's dominance of the animated film industry has been challenged, the result will certainly be a boon for people who enjoy animated films. It will mean a larger variety of story lines, more advanced computer animation and creators determined to push the limits of the genre. These are just a few of the developments we can expect from animated films in the future.

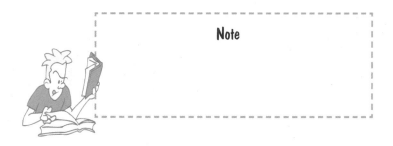

Note

True or False

—(1) When the first feature-length animated film was released, many production companies in Hollywood believed a cartoon film would fail.

—(2) When Disney had success with its first animated film, other companies in Hollywood started making animated films as well.

—(3) Disney made four popular animated films before "Beauty and the Beast."

—(4) Disney experienced a revival recently when a new group of artists joined the company.

—(5) Jeffrey Katzenberg holds the record for making the most profitable animated film ever.

—(6) Warner Brothers have been the biggest challenger to Disney in animation with their use of sports stars.

—(7) "The Prince of Egypt" was a typical Jeffrey Katzenberg film.

—(8) "The Price of Egypt" shocked the animated film industry in Hollywood because it was a film made for adults only.

—(9) Disney changed their style of animated film because DreamWorks' films were different.

—(10) It now seems that animated films in the future will probably use computers as characters.

Try This!

Each of the following descriptions is related to a film mentioned in the article. Write the film name beside each description.

———————————— Basketball hero meets the cartoon world.

———————————— She slept for 100 years until a handsome prince came along.

———————————— Religious cartoon like no other.

———————————— About a beautiful young woman and her short helpers.

———————————— What happens when children stop playing with their toys.

———————————— A famous story about a very famous bear.

———————————— The wooden boy who found it difficult to tell the truth.

———————————— Story about the animal king of the jungle.

———————————— A group of small farm animals decide it's time to escape.

———————————— About the funny genie who granted three wishes.

Key Words

animated *adj.* 栩栩如生的	dominance *n.* 優勢	partnership *n.* 合夥
blockbuster *n.* 賣座影片	dwarf *n.* 小矮人	release *v.* 上映；*n.* 初映
boon *n.* 益處	formula *n.* 公式	response *n.* 回應
box office *n.* 票房	genre *n.* 類型	revival *v.* 再興
consult *v.* 請教	groundbreaking *adj.* 破天荒	thrill *v.* 心情激動
credit *v.* 歸因於	offend *v.* 得罪	unfounded *adj.* 無根無據的

動畫電影

　　動畫電影，有時也稱做卡通影片，已經風行了六十餘年，而且大多數人只要一想到動畫電影，通常想到的都是迪士尼，因為迪士尼是動畫電影製作中，最原創也最具新意的。第一部長度達到影片標準的卡通影片，是1937年上映的《白雪公主》，上映當時，好萊塢其他的製片公司都認為卡通影片一定會失敗，不過事後證實他們的疑慮一點根據都沒有，《白雪公主》扶搖直上，受到全球觀眾的熱烈喜愛。1940年，迪士尼再接再厲，推出《木偶奇遇記》，之後，迪士尼電影工作室還上映了許多部影片，其中的著名影片包括1959年上映的《睡美人》，還有1977年的《小熊維尼》。

　　1990年代，迪士尼的動畫電影再次大放異彩，不少從事此業的人，都把這項成就的功勞歸給一群新進的藝術師，他們在1980年代末期加入迪士尼電影工作室，這群人中最重要的一位就是傑佛瑞·凱森柏。在他的領導之下，迪士尼製作了好多部的電影鉅片，像是1991年的《美女與野獸》，破天荒地運用了電腦動畫，讓全球觀眾大呼過癮；接下來的《阿拉丁》賺進兩億一千七百萬美元的票房，成為史上最賣座的電影；不過1994年，紀錄被凱森柏本人與其班底的《獅子王》打破了，《獅子王》至今仍是史上最賣座的動畫電影，票房收入達三億一千三百萬美元的天價。

　　好萊塢其他的製片工作室也決定來試一試動畫，華納兄弟製作了《威探闖通關》，接著又再推出《怪物奇兵》，這部電影融合了動畫以及籃球傳奇人物麥可·喬丹。之後，這一產業又有了巨變，傑佛瑞·凱森柏離開迪士尼，創立另一家新公司，與王牌導演史蒂芬·史匹柏、音樂製作人大衛·葛芬合夥，新公司名為「夢工場」。他們的第一部影片是《埃及王子》，好萊塢都給這部片嚇到了，因為凱森柏再度開創動畫電影的新風格，整部片拍起來比較像是給成人，而非給小孩看的。《埃及王子》費時四年拍攝，耗資約一億美元，夢工場請來四百二十五位藝術師參與這部影片，還請教了五百位左右的宗教領袖與專家，因為故事直接從聖經上節取下來，所以這部片拍出來之後，要不得罪人的困難度相當高。而迪士尼方面，則運用屢試不爽的拍片公式，再度製作動畫電影《玩具總動員》、《玩具總動員2》和《泰山》等片，都是很不錯的電影，票房也相當成功。夢工場也不甘示弱，1998年推出《小蟻雄兵》，之後在2000年又推出《落跑雞》。

　　而今迪士尼雄霸動畫電影工業的地位已經受到挑戰，這對於愛看動畫電影的人絕對有益，因為這意味著會有更多樣的故事情節、更先進的電腦動畫，創作者也會一心一意將這類影片推展到極致，而電影動畫的未來展望，絕對不只這些。

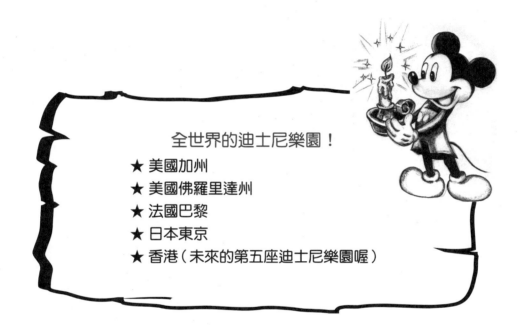

全世界的迪士尼樂園！
★ 美國加州
★ 美國佛羅里達州
★ 法國巴黎
★ 日本東京
★ 香港（未來的第五座迪士尼樂園喔）

The Flight of Mankind

自由飛翔，一直是人類的夢想。

The Flight of Mankind

People have always dreamed of being able to fly. For centuries, inventors and scientists made plans and attempts to fly, but all ended in failure and often death. However, everything changed at the beginning of the twentieth century. The key invention was the power engine and once this was utilized, men had the ability to propel aircraft into the sky. And since men   5 took off, they have seldom looked back.

Aviation history was made in an open field on the east coast of America. The year was 1903 and two brothers, Wilbur and Orville Wright completed the first ever powered flight. The distance traveled on this first occasion was only forty meters but that didn't matter. The technological breakthrough had   10 been made. Progress was rapid after this, and in 1909 a Frenchman named Louis Blériot safely flew forty-one kilometers from France to England. Between 1914 and 1918, the First World War provided more incentive for the development of aircraft. For the first time aircraft were used in warfare for bombing and transportation, and by the end of the war they had become   15 strong and reliable. The propeller became widely used on aircraft to act as a spinning wing to thrust the aircraft forward. Other improvements, such as new wing shapes, further progressed to maximize upward lift and sustained flight. In 1939 the world was again at war, and once again it was aircraft that were relied upon to cause widespread destruction. Technological   20 breakthroughs occurred frequently as better aircraft were continually designed by warring nations.

For the first half of the twentieth century, flying was only possible for air force pilots and the wealthy. Most people thought they would never get the chance to fly. This changed suddenly in 1950 with the development of the   25 modern jetliner. In 1958 the Boeing 707 was introduced to the world and commercial passenger flight began. Jetliners traveled at much greater speeds and at higher altitudes than before. By flying higher, jetliners could pass over the clouds and weather conditions that previously made air travel bumpy and unsafe. 30

By 1962, millions of people were traveling smoothly through the skies in pressurized cabins. The Boeing 747 began operating in 1970 and increased passenger capacity and the possible distances for travel. Today the Concorde with its thin pointed design is the fastest commercial aircraft. It flies from London and Paris to New York in four hours. In 2000, the European aircraft 35 designer Airbus announced their new aircraft called the A3XX. With passengers seated on two decks, this aircraft has the capacity to fly very long distances and carry over 500 people. The A3XX design is thought to be the beginning of a new age of mass passenger transportation.

Most commercial aircraft still use the same basic body designs as the 40 aircraft thirty years ago, with the major difference today being the way pilots use computers. In modern cockpits, computer screens with all the flight data are used instead of the hundreds of manual controls that pilots needed in the past. These days, aircraft travel has become so common that people rarely think twice about catching a plane. But we shouldn't become complacent 45 because only now are we actually living mankind's dream of flying across the sky.

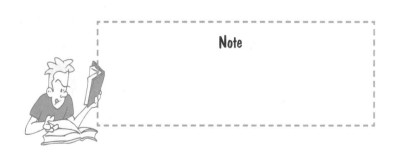

Note

Multiple Choice

—— 1. Many early attempts to fly ended in failure because ————.

    (A) all scientists had unrealistic designs

    (B) people at the time did not have enough desire to fly properly

    (C) the Wright Brothers hadn't been born yet

    (D) the required technology was not available

—— 2. The power engine was successfully used ————.

    (A) by the Wright Brothers in 1903

    (B) to advance the technology required to land safely

    (C) to utilize the benefits of flight

    (D) to make stronger spinning wing

—— 3. The early achievements in flying ————.

    (A) were all made in the United States

    (B) occurred in various countries at the start of the twentieth century

    (C) were incomparable to Louis Blériot's crossing of the English Channel

    (D) were all made by the Wright Brothers

—— 4. The First and Second World Wars ————.

    (A) were times of innovation in aircraft technology

    (B) were disastrous because so many aircraft were destroyed in battle

    (C) gave rise to complacent aircraft designs by the victors of the war

    (D) enabled people to escape by taking Boeing 747

—— 5. In the first half of the twentieth century, ————.

    (A) flying was only possible for air force pilots and the wealthy

    (B) jetliners had been developed and made air transportation prosper

    (C) the Boeing 747 began operating and increased passenger capacity

    (D) flying was not possible for air force pilots and the wealthy

—— 6. In the second half of the twentieth century, —————.

(A) the motivation for flying aircraft changed but not the basic aircraft design

(B) aircraft were used more for transportation than for war and entertainment

(C) the mistakes made in the first fifty years became obvious

(D) it was difficult to make any breakthrough in aviation

—— 7. Jetliners are the best aircraft for commercial passengers —————.

(A) because they can fly to any country in the world

(B) because of their ability to reach great speeds and high altitudes

(C) but some people believe they are not being properly utilized in modern life

(D) but they also result in more plane crashes than other kinds of aircraft

—— 8. The Concorde is mainly used —————.

(A) by the air force and sometimes used for commercial passengers

(B) to show what speeds are possible for modern aircraft

(C) to fly passengers over the Atlantic Ocean

(D) to carry cargoes across countries

—— 9. The new aircraft A3XX —————.

(A) can fly from London to Paris in only four hours

(B) is designed by the Wright Brothers

(C) can fly long distances and carry over 500 people

(D) has only a big deck which can carry over 500 people

—— 10. Many people are now complacent about flying because —————.

(A) pilots have an easy job with the computers they use

(B) it has become such a regular means of transportation

(C) it is such an incredible experience

(D) it makes wars become more destructive

Try This!

Use the following information and the article about flight to complete the time chart.

| Airbus A3XX | Boeing 707 | Blériot flies from France to England |
| Development of the jetliner | | End of the First World War |

Event	Year
Wright Brothers' first flight	_____
_____	1909
_____	1918
Start of the Second World War	1939
_____	_____
_____	1958
Millions of passengers flying	_____
Boeing 747	_____
_____	2000

Key Words

aircraft *n.* 飛機	incentive *n.* 誘因	propeller *n.* 螺旋槳
air force *n.* 空軍	jetliner *n.* 噴射客機	rapid *adj.* 快速的
altitude *n.* 高度	lift *n.* 上升	reliable *adj.* 可靠的
aviation *n.* 飛行	mankind *n.* 人類	smoothly *adv.* 平穩地
bomb *v.* 轟炸	manual *adj.* 手動的	spin *v.* 旋轉
bumpy *adj.* 顛簸搖晃的	maximize *v.* 增加至極限	sustain *v.* 維持
cabin *n.* 機艙	pointed *adj.* 尖的	thrust *v.* 推
cockpit *n.* 駕駛艙	pressurize *v.* 使氣壓正常	utilize *v.* 利用
complacent *adj.* 得意的	previously *adv.* 先前	warfare *n.* 戰爭
deck *n.* 層	propel *v.* 推進	wealthy *adj.* 有錢的

人類飛行史

　　人類一直夢想著能夠飛翔。幾百年來，發明家和科學家做了各種設計和嘗試，希望能夠飛翔，不過最後都失敗了，而且往往因此喪命。然而，二十世紀初期，一切有了改觀，最關鍵的發明就是動力引擎，利用這項發明，人類就可以將飛機推升到天空，而人類一旦起飛之後，就很少再回頭看了。

　　飛行的歷史是在美國東岸的曠野上展開的，那年是1903年，萊特兄弟——威爾伯和奧維爾兩人，完成史上首次的動力飛行，雖然頭一遭的飛航距離只有四十公尺，但是沒有關係，因為這已造就了科技上的突破，之後的進展便一日千里。1909年，法國人路易・布萊里奧安全地從法國飛抵英國，全長四十一公里。1914到1918年間，第一次世界大戰使得飛機的發展有了更大的誘因，飛機也首次用於戰爭中，用來轟炸或是運輸；到了大戰末期，飛機更為堅固，也更可靠。螺旋槳廣泛地用在飛機上，當作螺旋翼將飛機向前推進。而其他的改良，像是機翼的形狀翻新，更進一步將升空能力及續航力提升至最高限度。1939年，全世界再次開戰，飛機也再度受到利用，造成遍地的破壞，不過正因為交戰國不斷設計更好的飛機，所以科技才能常常有所突破。

　　二十世紀前半葉，只有空軍飛行員和有錢人才可能搭飛機，極大多數的人都覺得自己一輩子不會有這個機會。不過到了1950年，新式的噴射客機改良後，這種情形馬上就改變了。1958年，波音707問世，開始了商務航空，而且噴射客機的飛行速度增加，飛行高度也提升了，這樣一來，就可以飛到雲層之上，擺脫原本不良的天候，飛行就不再會搖晃危險。

1962年之前，就已經有幾百萬人坐在壓力艙中，安穩地飛過天際。波音747於1970年開始營運，不只載客量增加，航程也加到最長。現今的協和號設計得又尖又細，是速度最快的商務客機，從倫敦或巴黎起飛，不到四個小時就能飛抵紐約。西元2000年，歐洲的飛機製造商空中巴士宣布，他們的新型飛機定名為A3XX，乘客坐在兩層機艙之中，飛機可長程飛行，而且能載運五百多名的乘客，許多人認為，A3XX的設計開啟了大眾運輸的新頁。

大多數商用客機，其機身的主體設計還是跟三十年前一樣，最大的不同在於現今的駕駛員都會利用電腦來開飛機。現代的駕駛艙中，電腦螢幕上都是飛航的資料，而以前的駕駛員用的是幾百個手動的操控裝置。近年來，搭飛機有如家常便飯，一般人幾乎想都不想就搭飛機，不過我們也不要太過得意，因為也是要到現在，我們才真正實現人類飛越蒼穹的夢想。

Unit

30 *Snow Skiing*

Yes! 有機會一定要親身體驗滑雪的自由暢快喔！

Snow Skiing

Hans Schmidt is a twenty-five-year-old skiing instructor from Austria. This is a story he told about his life of skiing.

"Like many people in Europe, I see snow almost every winter. My hometown of Salzburg is actually surrounded by mountains, so my family and friends all consider it normal to ski. Some of my earliest memories from childhood are taking ski lifts to the top of a mountain, and then skiing back down with my parents. When I was a teenager, I used to ski with my friends after school, mainly cross country and sometimes downhill. And now that I am working, I still get to ski every day. That's because my job is a ski instructor; I teach people how to ski."

"Often I teach people who have never skied before. I start them off on a gentle slope about ten meters long. We practice the fundamentals of turning and stopping, and once I am satisfied with their progress we move on. For the beginner, catching ski lifts can be difficult. They have to line up with other skiers and get onto a moving lift as it approaches. But after a few embarrassing moments, they manage to get on and off at the right time. Then comes the biggest test. They stand at the top of the slope, get their skis straight, bend their knees and push off. Often they go for about thirty meters before losing balance and falling. But at this stage, they don't go fast so it's not too dangerous. I just keep encouraging my students to be persistent and brave."

"Over the years I've taught thousands of people how to ski. If people want to just get down an easy slope without falling, then it will only take them one day of practice. On the second and third days, they can explore other slopes on the mountain and practice their turns. And if they stay for a week, they will actually be quite good skiers. In this sense, skiing is an easy sport to learn. Of course once a skier gets more advanced, there are many things to learn about technique. But if he or she just wants to have fun and ski down a slope without crashing, then there is not much difficulty at all."

"I love skiing because of the freedom it gives you. When the snow is   30
fresh and soft like powder, it's wonderful to make big arch turns and see the
snow spray off the edges of your skis. These days many people are
snowboarding which looks like great fun with all the jumps and turns they
make. But personally I think downhill skiing on traditional skis has more
style. Skiing is also a sport you can enjoy all around the world. Europe,   35
Canada, the USA, Japan and New Zealand are ideal places to downhill ski
because of their excellent slopes and breathtaking mountain scenery. And
even after a day of skiing, there is plenty to enjoy. What could be better than
returning to your hotel, relaxing in a sauna and eating a warm meal in front of
a fireplace?"   40

Note

True or False

——(1) It's normal for people like Hans to ski because his home is near mountains.

——(2) Hans teaches people how to ski as a part-time job.

——(3) Ski instructors aren't those who have little skiing experience.

——(4) When people learn to ski, they start by learning the fundamentals of turning and getting off ski lifts.

——(5) The first time people ski on a real slope, they usually fall without hurting themselves.

——(6) Hans believes learning the basics of snow skiing is actually quite easy.

——(7) For the advanced skier, it takes about a week to learn good technique.

——(8) Skiing gives you a feeling of freedom when the snow is fresh and soft like powder.

——(9) Hans prefers snowboarding to downhill skiing on traditional skis because snowboarding has more style.

——(10) People can only downhill ski and snowboard where there are mountains and slopes.

Try This!

Read the following clues and match them with these activities and sports.

> skiing   parachuting   football   bungee jumping   rollerblading   surfing
> baseball   tennis   horse riding   golf   swimming   table tennis

1) Play against another person on a court ———————

2) On a mountain during winter ———————

3) In parks or on the streets with wheels on your feet ———————

4) Off a bridge with a cord attached to your back ———————

5) You have to get wet for this ———————

6) Throwing and hitting with a team for nine innings ———————

7) Jump from an aircraft and slowly fall to the earth ———————

8) Move along on the back of a large animal ———————

9) In the ocean, riding waves that break close to the beach ———————

10) With ten other players all trying to kick the ball into the goal ———————

11) Fast game between singles or doubles on an elevated surface ———————

12) Hit a little ball until it falls in a hole ———————

Key Words

arch *n.* 弧形	fireplace *n.* 壁爐	sauna *n.* 三溫暖
beginner *n.* 初學者	fundamental *n.* 基礎	ski *v.* 滑雪；*n.* 滑雪屐
breathtaking *adj.* 令人驚嘆的	instructor *n.* 教練	ski lift *n.* 雪地纜車
crash *v.* 跌撞	persistent *adj.* 堅持的	slope *n.* 斜坡
downhill *adj.* 下坡的	powder *n.* 粉末	snowboard *n.* 滑雪板
embarrassing *adj.* 尷尬的	Salzburg 薩爾堡	spray *v.* 產生浪花

滑雪

　　漢斯・史密特今年二十五歲，是一位奧地利滑雪教練，以下內容是他所口述有關自己的滑雪生涯。

　　「跟歐洲多數人一樣，我幾乎每年冬天都看得到雪。我的家鄉薩爾堡四周都是山，所以我的家人和朋友都認為滑雪沒有什麼稀奇，我還記得小時候，會搭雪地纜車到山頂上去，然後再跟我爸媽一起從山上滑下來。十多歲時，我放學後常常和同學一起滑雪，大部分都是在田野間滑雪，有時候也會從山上往下滑；而我現在已經在工作了，還是天天滑雪，因為我的職業就是滑雪教練，教別人滑雪。」

　　「通常我教的人以前都沒滑過雪，所以都從較平的斜坡開始，長度差不多十公尺，我們練習一些轉彎、煞車等基本動作，只要他們的進度能讓我滿意，就練習下一個動作。對初學者來說，搭纜車可能不容易，他們必須和其他滑雪的人一起排隊，還得趁移動中的纜車靠過來時就坐上去，但是丟臉幾次之後，就能抓對上下纜車的時間了。接下來就是最大的考驗，他們要站在山頂上，穿好滑雪屐，曲膝，然後出發。通常前三十公尺都還能保持平衡，可是後來就會滑倒了，不過這個階段他們滑得也不是很快，所以沒有什麼危險性。我會一直鼓勵我的學生要勇敢、要再接再厲。」

　　「這麼多年來，我也教了好幾千人滑雪，一般人假使只求滑下一個不太陡的斜坡，而且不要跌倒的話，那只要練習一天就可以了；第二天和第三天，他們可以到山上其他的斜坡玩一玩，練一練轉彎；要是他們待上一個禮拜的話，就可以滑得很不錯了，這樣說來，滑雪算是很容易學的運動。當然啦，滑雪的人想要再進一步的話，技巧方面還有很多東西可以學；如果只是想要玩得高興，從山坡上滑下來不跌倒就好的話，那就沒什麼太大的困難。」

　　「我很喜歡滑雪，因為感覺很自由。雪剛下沒多久，還軟得像粉的時候，來個大轉彎，看看滑雪屐兩側飛濺的雪花，真是棒極了！最近很多人都在玩滑雪板，可以跳啊、轉啊，看起來很好玩，不過我個人認為，穿傳統的滑雪屐，再從山坡上滑下來，別有一番風味。滑雪這項運動，世界各地都可以進行，歐洲、加拿大、美國、日本、紐西蘭都是滑雪的理想去處，因為這些地方的滑坡都很棒，山景也是令人嘆為觀止。而且就算滑雪滑了一天之後，還有很多其他好玩的，回到旅館，可以洗個三溫暖放鬆一下，然後再到壁爐前面吃頓熱騰騰的晚餐，有什麼比這更愜意的呢？

漫談滑雪

滑雪是一項既浪漫又刺激的運動。它起源於北歐的挪威，早在幾千年前，當人們的生產條件還很落後時，人類為了在惡劣的自然環境中生存，發明了可以替代行走的滑雪板，它的應用使得人們可以在浩瀚森林中任意馳騁追尋獵物。

滑雪運動可分為越野滑雪、高山滑雪兩大類。越野滑雪起源於北歐的挪威，主要在平原或地形起伏不大的丘陵地帶發展，也是主要的代步工具；高山滑雪起源於歐洲阿爾卑斯山區，所以也稱阿爾卑斯滑雪，主要在地形起伏較大的山區發展。不過，這兩種滑雪運動所使用的滑雪器材和滑雪技巧卻完全不同。

Answers

1. The Internet

D B A A C A B A D C

1) Jessica 2) I–Space Company
3) EveCommerce 4) YourNet Inc.
5) I–Space Company 6) Jessica
7) Jessica 8) EveCommerce

2. Exchange Student

T T F T T T F F F F

Correct answers: 2), 3), 5), 8)

3. Christopher Columbus

B A D A D D B C A C

America, Italy, Africa, Spain,
Portugal, China, Europe, Asia

4. Australia

T F F T F T T F T F

Perth, Sydney, Aboriginal people,
Melbourne, British people, summer,
sport, north, crocodile

5. Triathlon

D C C A A A B A C D

1. triathlon 2. concentrate 3. modify
4. competitor 5. draining 6. stages
7. legs

6. "Twist and Shout"

F T F T T T F T F T

John, Paul, George and Ringo

thick black hair

~~fashionable musicians and hairdressers~~

young men from working class backgrounds

innovative

created the "Beatlemania" phenomenon

world-famous in the 1960's

~~famous for their music and painting~~

~~no longer popular~~

screaming fans

~~kept making the same style of music~~

greater chart success in the USA than any

other band

7. Making Movies

T T F T F F F T F F

5 2 8 6 3 9 1 4 7

8. Earthquakes

T T T F F F F T T F

1. fire 2. post 3. home 4. hand
5. line 6. top 7. frame 8. day

9. The Ancient Egyptians

D C A B B A B A D C

burial ———— chamber
dead ———— soul
leather ———— sandals
black ———— hair
massive ———— tombs
ancient ———— Egyptians
rich ———— soil
modern ———— world
common ———— people
lip ———— powder
skilled ———— craftsman

10.Working Part-time

F F F T F F T T T

Mon.	Class	Class	Class	Class	Free	Work	Work
Tue.	Class	Class	Class	Class	Free	Study	Study
Wed.	Class	Class	Class	Class	Free	Work	Work
Thu.	Free	Free	Free	Free	Free	Study	Study
Fri.	Class	Class	Class	Class	Gym	Work	Work

11.Dear Jane Sanders

A C B D B B B D D A

reason personal doubt enthusiasm

12.The Channel Tunnel

T T F T F T T F F F

Chalk Rock Creates Headache for Drillers (*3*)

International Airport Chosen Instead of Terminal (*wrong*)

Not One...But THREE (*2*)

Engineers Agree Channel Tunnel is "Possible" (*1*)

Eurotunnel Chooses France Over England (*4*)

Passengers Agree on Tunnel Dimensions (*wrong*)

Politicians Pleased With Their "Tunnel Vision" (*wrong*)

Tunnel Dream Comes True (*5*)

13.Hong Kong

B C B C A D D B A A

(Low taxation rates make Hong Kong a financial center)

(English language understood by Hong Kong residents)

(Political decision making from 1898–1997)

(The decision to build the new Hong Kong airport)

14.Choosing a New Camera

F F T F T F T F F T

1) automatic 2) camera 3) flash 4) lens

5) red-eye reduction 6) shutter 7) self-timer

8) zoom 9) photographs 10) adjust

15.Beach Excursion

C A C B A B A C D D

From lines 1~23

excursion expect rented relaxed

normal scattered marine crucial

From lines 24~43

garbage ecosystem starve enthusiastic

volunteer collect task disposing

16.Good English

D A D A A D B C B B

1) email 2) business 3) job interview

4) novel 5) letter 6) newspaper

17.Australian Aboriginal People

T F T T T F T F F F

1) theory 2) fact 3) fact 4) theory

5) fact   6) fact 7) fact 8) theory

18.The Titanic

C A A B D B C C B A

2) help 3) reveal 4) middle 5) die

6) spear 7) launch 8) stop   9) signal

10) newspaper

19. Environmental Damage

T T T F F T T F F T

<u>Cause</u>: factory contamination,
　　　car pollution,
　　　forests chopped down,
　　　burning fossil fuels

<u>Effect</u>: powerful storms,
　　　global warming,
　　　floods,
　　　poor soil

<u>Solution</u>: use public transportation,
　　　use clean energy,
　　　reduce consumption,
　　　recycle waste

20. Rip Van Winkle

B C C B A D A A C D

√× 　√× 　×√ 　×√ 　√× 　×√

21. Computer Games

T T T F T F T F F F

1) guarantee, Toronto　2) personal computer
3) <u>www.supergame.ca</u>　4) trade
5) Games Superstore　6) virtual reality

22. The Story of Elvis Presley

D B C A C B A C A C

1C, 2A, 3E, 4G, 5B, 6D, 7F

23. The Work of Amnesty International

F T F F T T T F F T

AI: (2), (3), (5), (7), (9)

24. Thailand

C B B A D A C B C D

	TC	TP	FI
Sukhothai		√	
Chinese culture			√
Thai Buddhism	√		
Chiang Mai		√	
Phuket		√	
Inward Tourism	√		
King of Thailand	√		
Thai script	√		
Burmese armies			√
Bangkok		√	
Thai food	√		
Indian culture			√
Ayuthaya		√	

25. The European Union

A B A A C B C D D D

Influenced	European	Same
yes	border control	
	languages	yes
yes	money system	
yes	international trade	
	country leadership	yes
yes	jobs and work	
	cultural differences	yes
	geography	yes
	population size	yes
yes	population spread	
yes	European cooperation	

26. Claude Monet and the Impressionists

T F T F F T F T T F

<u>Form lines 1~20</u>

　　western, imprecise, quick, foreground,
　　hard, difficult, best, young, same, sell

From lines 21~43
innovative, before, gradually, wider,
successful, confirmed, finally, live, secure,
bought

9) surfing   10) football   11) table tennis
12) golf

27. The Sixties Generation

D A C B A D A D A A

√ × × √ × √ × × √ √ × √

28. Animated Films

T F F T T F F F F F

Space Jam

Sleeping Beauty

The Prince of Egypt

Snow White and the Seven Dwarfs

Toy Story, Toy Story2

Winnie the Pooh

Pinocchio

The Lion King

Chicken Run

Aladdin

29. The Flight of Mankind

D A B A A B B C C B

Event: Blériot flies from France to England

End of the First World War

Development of the jetliner

Boeing 707

Airbus A3XX

Year: 1903, 1950, 1962, 1970

30. Snow Skiing

T F T F T T F F F T

1) tennis   2) skiing   3) rollerblading

4) bungee jumping   5) swimming

6) baseball   7) parachuting   8) horse riding